P9-EEN-905

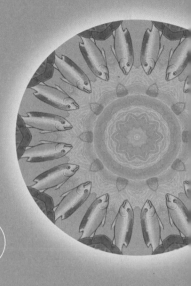

What parts of the front
cover picture do you see
in the design to the left?

How many starfish parts
can you find?

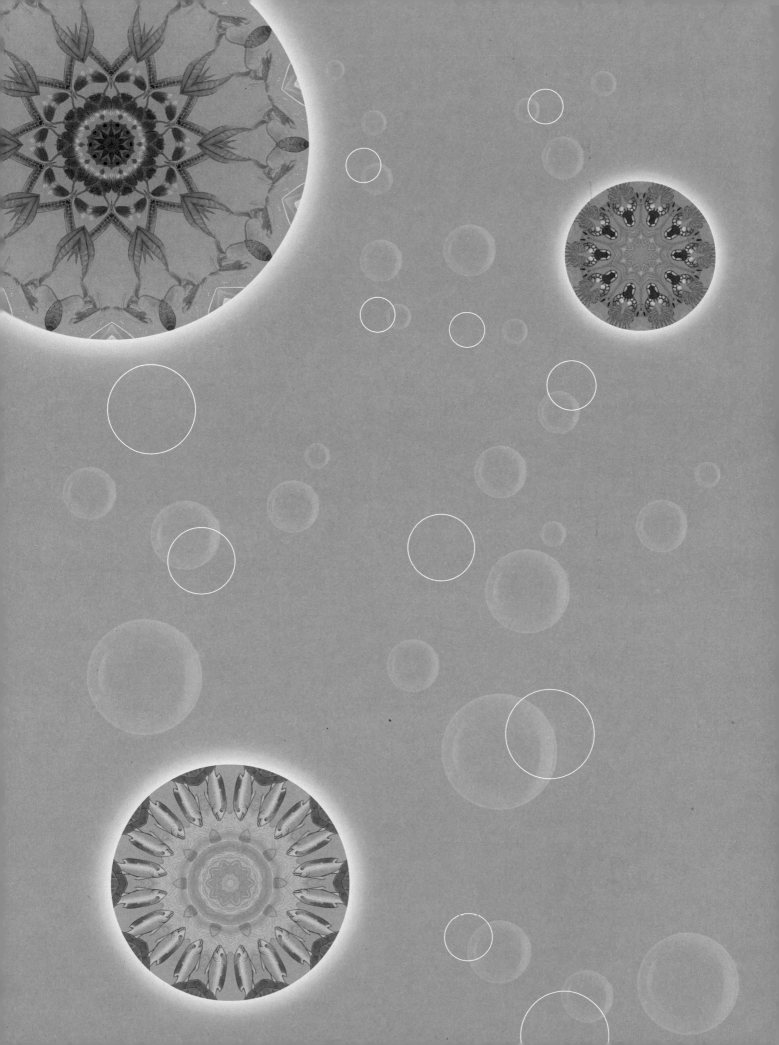

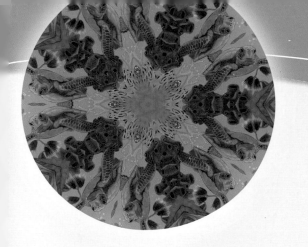

Literacy by Design™

Sourcebook
Volume 1

Program Authors

Linda Hoyt

Michael Opitz

Robert Marzano

Sharon Hill

Yvonne Freeman

David Freeman

Rigby®

A Harcourt Achieve Imprint

www.Rigby.com

1-800-531-5015

Welcome to Literacy by Design,
Where Reading Is...

Discovering

Imagining

Questioning

Literacy by Design: Sourcebook Volume 1
Grade 3

ISBN-13: 978-1-4189-4037-9
ISBN-10: 1-4189-4037-2

Printed in China
1A 2 3 4 5 6 7 8 985 13 12 11 10 09 08 07

Thinking

Exploring

UNIT People and Places

iv

GREETINGS FROM
NEW MEXICO
USA 37

THEME ② **Life in Many Places** Pages 34–63

Modeled Reading

Shared Reading

Interactive Reading

v

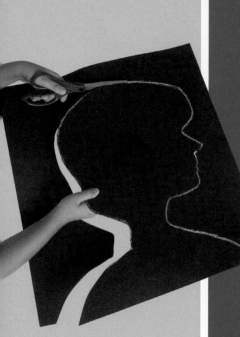

UNIT ▸ *Thinking Like a Scientist*

THEME ③ **What Is Light?** Pages 66–95

Modeled Reading

Shared Reading

Interactive Reading

THEME ④ How Does Electricity Work? Pages 96–125

UNIT Then and Now

THEME ⑥ **Roads to Travel On** Pages 158–187

Modeled Reading

Shared Reading

Interactive Reading

UNIT Forces of Nature

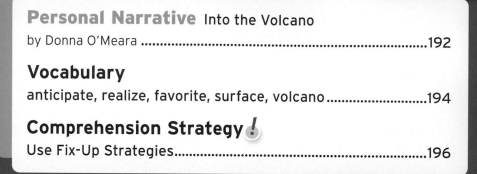

THEME **7** **On Moving Ground** Pages 190–219

1

Sugaring Off, 1955
Anna Mary Robertson
"Grandma" Moses (1860–1961)

People and Places

Viewing

The artist, Grandma Moses, often painted scenes of daily life in the country. This painting shows people collecting sap, or "sugar" from maple trees. They are boiling the sap to make syrup and other products, in a process called "sugaring off."

1. How would you describe the people in this community?

2. What activities show that the community is working together?

3. What kind of place does the painting show? What clues from the painting helped you decide?

4. How is the life in the painting similar to and different from life in the place where you live?

In This UNIT

In this unit, you will read about how people in communities work together and what life is like in different places.

Contents

Modeled Reading

Shared Reading

Interactive Reading

Genre
Personal Narrative

OGBO

Sharing Life in an African Village

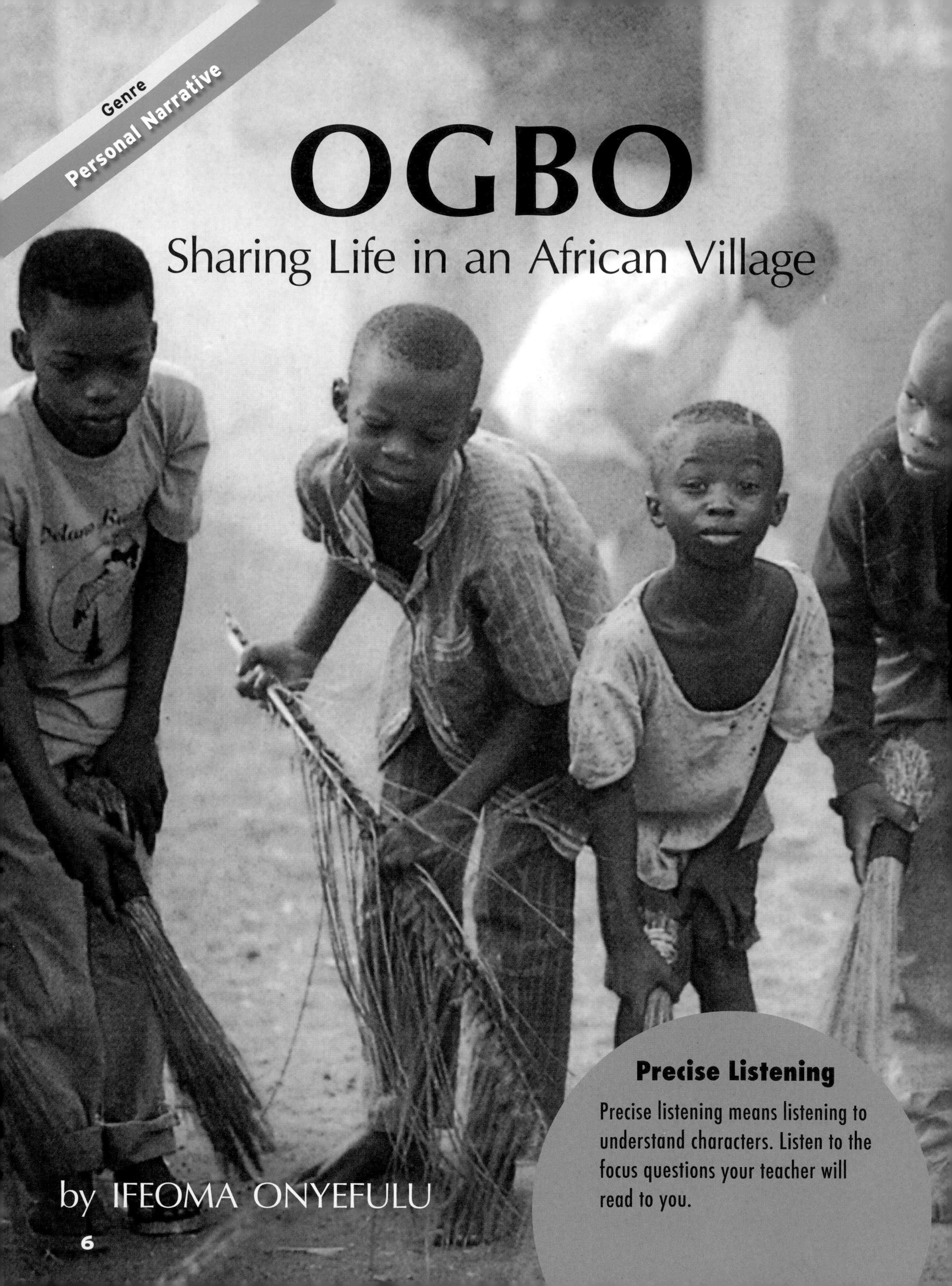

by IFEOMA ONYEFULU

Precise Listening

Precise listening means listening to understand characters. Listen to the focus questions your teacher will read to you.

Community Murals

A mural is a painting on a wall. Making murals is one way to **celebrate** a community.

A famous mural artist helped a community make a **decision** about the message of *"Our Community Mural."* The painting shows how people in a community can help and **protect** one another.

*This "Healing Mural" is in a hospital. It gives **comfort** to the children who stay there. Doctors, nurses, and patients helped **develop** this mural.*

Structured Vocabulary Discussion

Finish each of the following sentences using what you know about each vocabulary word.

- We had a reason to *celebrate* because . . .

- Two things that bring me *comfort* are . . .

- I *protect* myself from getting sick by . . .

- A hard *decision* for me is . . .

- In order to *develop* my musical ability, I could . . .

Throughout the week, add to your vocabulary journal entries. Record new insights and other words that relate to this week's vocabulary.

Picture It

Copy this word chart into your vocabulary journal. List a **decision** that you have made at home or school.

decision
when to do homework

Copy this word wheel into your vocabulary journal. Write the first words that you think of when you see the word **comfort**.

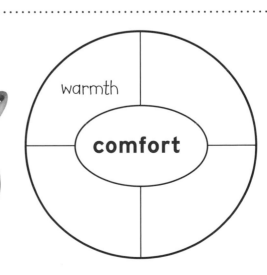

warmth

comfort

Comprehension Strategy

Make Connections

A **CONNECTION** is a link between two ideas.

Connect ideas in your reading to what you already know.

TURN AND TALK Listen as your teacher reads from *Ogbo: Sharing Life in an African Village* and models how to make connections. Then with a partner discuss answers to these questions.

• What do you know about a community?

• Does the *ogbo* remind you of community in your life? Why or why not?

TAKE IT WITH YOU When you make connections, you use what you already know to understand the ideas in your reading better. As you read, make connections to your own life. Think about things you have read, heard, seen, or done before. Use a chart like the one below to make connections as you read.

In the Text	This Reminds Me Of...
"In Awkuzu, every child belongs to an ogbo, together with all the other children born within a five-year period."	An ogbo is like a family. I have a family.
"Everyone has a friend; no one is born alone."	In my neighborhood, I have friends. My neighborhood is like an ogbo.

A Small Town with a Big Idea

by John Andrews

Smalltown was just like its name. It was so small, it didn't even appear on maps.

"We need to put Smalltown on the map!" declared Mayor Maple at the town meeting. "How can we get people to notice us? Let's think big!"

Farmer Johnnycake said the town needed a web site. Jack Flap said the town should host a monster truck show. Then Linda had an idea. Linda was a third grader.

"Next week is our town pancake breakfast," she said. "Let's make the world's largest pancake!"

"Now that's a big idea," said Mayor Maple. Everyone agreed.

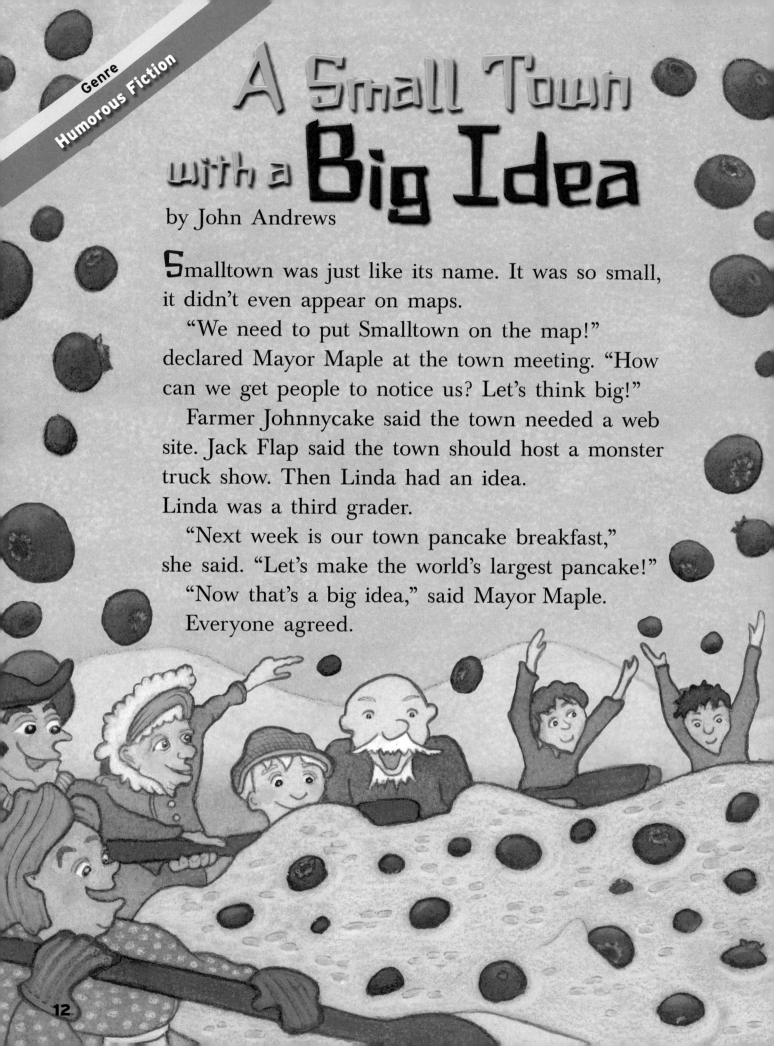

The townspeople discovered the record-holding pancake was forty-nine feet across.

"We'll make ours fifty feet!" announced Mayor Maple. "Who has a pan that big?"

Jack Flap said they could use the top of his silo as a pan. Electricians turned it into a hot plate.

Everyone worked together to make the batter. Finally they poured it. The townspeople gasped. The batter poured right over the sides of the pan!

With boat oars, everyone pushed batter toward the center of the pan. Now the pancake was too small. The pancake was browning quickly. It stretched to only forty feet across—not a record.

Suddenly there was a shower of blueberries. The third graders had picked blueberries for the breakfast. They tossed them on the pancake. "It's the world's largest *blueberry* pancake!" cried Linda.

Now Smalltown would surely be put on the map.

Community Calendar

September 11th
Open House at Town Animal Shelter

Come adopt a pet today! We have many cats and dogs waiting for good homes. We'll also help you train your pet.

September 13th
School-Community Meeting

This month's meeting for parents, teachers, and students will be at the town library. Help us plan a carnival. We will be raising money for class field trips.

September 15th
Safety Day at the Police Station

Do you want to know how to keep your family safe? Learn how to put in a car seat, lock up your home, and get a neighborhood watch started.

September 16th
Mexican Independence Day Parade

Come to Town Square to celebrate Mexican Independence Day. Learn about Mexico's rich history. Watch the colorful parade. Enjoy the food and fun.

Short Vowels

Activity One

About Short Vowels

Sometimes the vowels *a*, *e*, *i*, *o*, and *u* make a short vowel sound. For example, the word *sat* has the short *a* sound. Here are some words with short vowel sounds: *plan, Sam, test, stretch, mint, insist, clock, not, must, trunk*. As your teacher reads *Community Calendar*, listen for words with short vowel sounds.

Short Vowels in Context

With a group, read *Community Calendar*. Work with your group to find words with short vowel sounds. Write separate lists for short *a*, *e*, *i*, *o*, and *u* words.

Activity Two

Explore Words Together

luck	blink
batter	mess
lag	stock

Work with a partner to think of more short vowel words. Start with the words on the right. For each word, replace the short vowel with a different short vowel. Then write a list of the new short vowel words for each vowel sound.

Activity Three

Explore Words in Writing

Write sentences about a community activity. Use at least one short vowel word in each sentence. Then exchange your sentences with a partner. Circle the words with the short vowel sound in each other's sentences.

Special Olympics
Where the World Comes Together

by Rana Strong

A Special Olympics Race

Go for the gold! That's what Special Olympics means. Special Olympics is a sports program that gives opportunities to people who have physical and mental challenges.

Members of Special Olympics face more challenges learning and doing things than others their age. The message of the program is that all people deserve a chance to play sports and have fun.

There are more than two million Special Olympic athletes around the world. They live in more than 150 countries.

> Can you think of another time when athletes from all over the world come together?

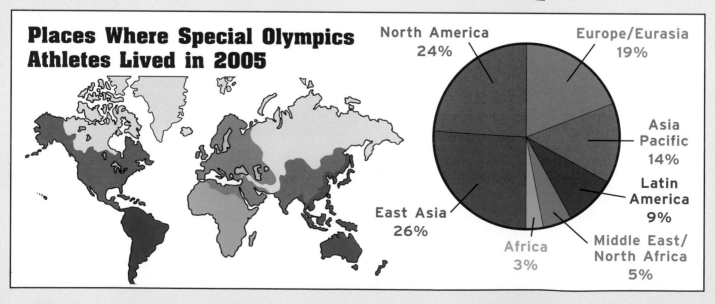

Places Where Special Olympics Athletes Lived in 2005

- North America 24%
- Europe/Eurasia 19%
- Asia Pacific 14%
- Latin America 9%
- Middle East/North Africa 5%
- Africa 3%
- East Asia 26%

What are the Special Olympics World Games?

The World Games are special times. People from all over the world meet for the games. World Games happen every two years in a different country. There are Summer and Winter Games. Children who are eight and older may play in the official games. Adults of all ages also train and play.

What kinds of sports do the Special Olympics athletes play?

The athletes play more than twenty-five kinds of sports. Some of the winter sports are skiing, skating, and snowboarding. For the Summer Games, some of the athletes play basketball, soccer, and tennis.

What have you heard about the Special Olympics?

Downhill Skiing

17

How do athletes get ready for the World Games?

The athletes train hard all year long. They establish a healthy lifestyle. They eat good food, exercise, and get plenty of rest. The athletes practice their sports. They learn the best ways to play. They learn not to give up easily. Their hard work will take them to the Special Olympics World Games.

What are the World Games like?

The World Games begin with an amazing opening ceremony. Athletes from each country march into the stadium. The sports events are exciting. In the power lifting, for example, the athletes show great strength. In team sports, the play is fierce! Thousands of fans cheer on their country's athletes. Each event ends with a medal ceremony.

Read, Cover, Remember, Retell Technique With a partner, take turns reading as much text as you can cover with your hand. Then cover up what you read and retell the information to your partner.

The Olympic Flame

Do you know any athletes that train like the athletes in the Special Olympics? What do they do?

Power Lifting

Are there rules that Special Olympics athletes must follow?

Yes. Athletes agree to many important rules. One rule is to show care and kindness to other players at all times. Athletes also promise to practice and prepare. They agree to listen to coaches. The athletes promise to do their best.

How do Special Olympics make a difference?

When the athletes train and compete, they make their minds and bodies stronger. They learn how to set goals. Then they work to reach their goals. Their hard work pays off in many ways. The athletes learn the feeling of being proud. They learn how to win and lose. They also make great friends with other athletes.

Have you ever set a goal and reached it like the athletes in the Special Olympics? Explain.

A Coach and Athletes

19

How is the community involved in Special Olympics?

Almost one million people give their time to help Special Olympics. Many others donate money. The program depends on help from the community. Volunteers coach, referee, and keep score. Others help the athletes by cheering them on.

Everyone wins by supporting the Special Olympics. Fans get to see amazing athletic competitions. They can also learn a lot from the athletes. Athletes teach others about pride, hard work, and being a good sport. Just think of the Special Olympics athlete's oath, "Let me win. But if I cannot win, let me be brave in the attempt."

What volunteers in your community do you know? How do they help?

A Special Olympics Race

A Medal Winner

Lighting the Special Olympics Flame

Think and Respond

Reflect and Write

- You and your partner took turns reading and retelling sections of *Special Olympics: Where the World Comes Together*. Discuss what you and your partner retold.

- On one side of an index card, write a connection you made with the passage. On the other side, write how this connection helped you understand what you read.

Short Vowels in Context

Search *Special Olympics: Where the World Comes Together* to find words with short vowels. Make lists of short vowel words for *a*, *e*, *i*, *o*, and *u*. Then compare your lists with a partner's.

Turn and Talk

MAKE CONNECTIONS

Discuss with a partner what you have learned so far about how to make connections as you read.

- How does making connections help you learn more from what you read?

With a partner, reread page 19. Think of a connection between Special Olympics and something you have done. Share your connection with your partner.

Critical Thinking

With a partner, discuss why you think Special Olympics were formed. Write a list of ways Special Olympics help people. Then answer these questions.

- How do you think athletes feel when they compete in the Special Olympics? How do you think the volunteers feel?

- How are the Special Olympics an example of a community?

BE A PART OF HISTORY!

COME SEE THE OREGON TRAIL WAGON TRAIN

October 6, 12 noon

Come to the community event of the year! An old wagon train will roll into town. The wagons will drive along part of the Oregon Trail that once passed through our town in 1846. Back then, families gave up their old **lifestyle** to join the wagon trail. They wanted to **establish** new homes in the West. The wagons had everything needed to set up a new **household**.

Be sure to **arrive** early to see all the action. We'll have music, dancing, a cookout, and wagon races. You can try your luck panning for gold. You can say hello to the live animals. We'll have activities to **appeal** to all!

Structured Vocabulary Discussion

When your teacher says a vocabulary word, you and your partner should each write down the first words you think of on a piece of paper. When your teacher says, "Stop," exchange papers with your partner and explain the words on your lists to each other.

Throughout the week, add to your vocabulary journal entries. Record new insights and other words that relate to this week's vocabulary.

Picture It

Copy this word organizer into your vocabulary journal. List things about your community that **appeal** to you.

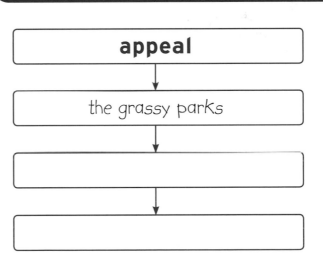

Copy this word web into your vocabulary journal. Fill in the circles with words that describe your **household.**

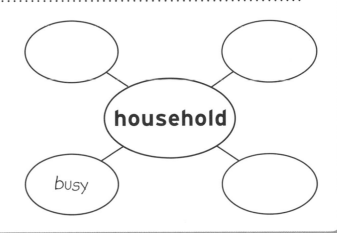

No Place like Greenville!

by Ted Louis

There's no city or town
from the East to the West
that is finer than mine.
Greenville's surely the best!

Our town hall is grander
than a palace in Rome.
Yet that's not the reason
that I boast of my home.

I'd say that our parks,
have more trees than a jungle.
Still, the reason I love
my town is more humble.

Though Loch Ness is famous,
our lake is more so.
Its secrets amaze,
and continue to grow.

While we have a million shops,
and not one is the same,
there's more to it than that,
so I'll have to explain.

In each Greenville household,
folks are honest and true.
It's the community's people
that make me feel as I do!

The Potlatch Party

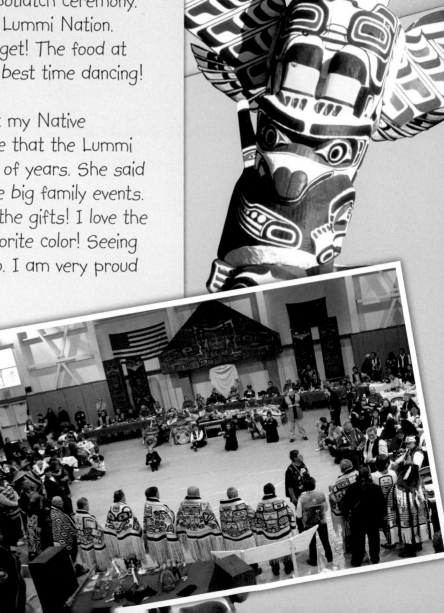

May 31st

Dear Uncle Bob,

Thanks for asking us to your potlatch ceremony. I always have fun when I visit the Lummi Nation. But this was a day I will never forget! The food at the feast was delicious. I had the best time dancing! It was great to see my cousins.

It was fun to learn more about my Native American ancestors. Mom told me that the Lummi have had potlatches for hundreds of years. She said our people have them to celebrate big family events.

It is funny that the hosts give the gifts! I love the vest you gave me. Violet is my favorite color! Seeing the new totem pole was great, too. I am very proud to be a part of the family.

Love,

Verna

At a Potlach, Northwest Native Americans celebrate a family event such as a birth or marriage.

Initial Consonants

Potlach Basket

Activity One

About Initial Consonants

The letters *b*, *d*, *f*, *m*, and *v* are all consonants. When a consonant comes at the beginning of a word, it is called an initial consonant. For example, *m* is the initial consonant in the word *move*. Choose one of the initial consonants *b*, *d*, *f*, *m*, or *v*. As your teacher reads *The Potlatch Party*, listen for words that begin with that letter.

Initial Consonants in Context

Read the letter with a partner. Work together to find words that begin with *b*, *d*, *f*, *m*, and *v*. Record these words in a list.

Activity Two

Explore Words Together

With a partner read the words on the right. Think of other words that can go with each word and that begin with *b*, *d*, *f*, *m*, or *v*. For example, you could write *frisky dog* or *dog bone*. List each pair and underline the initial consonant of each word.

dog	mice
blueberry	vase
field	day

Activity Three

Explore Words in Writing

Write sentences that tell about ways you can help your community. Use at least five words that begin with *b*, *d*, *f*, *m*, or *v*. When you have finished writing, share your sentences with a partner.

Genre
Realistic Fiction

THE GREAT Butterfly Flutterby

by Margaret Fetty

Liz and Ben rode their bikes through Lakewood. The whole town was in a flutter. Every one was getting ready for the Monarch Butterfly Festival. Bright orange and black butterfly flags hung from the light poles. Mr. Ice was setting up his nectar snow cone booth. The carnival rides were ready. Only one thing was missing— the monarch butterflies!

Mayor Rogers waved to Liz and Ben. "Have you spotted any monarchs yet?" Mayor Rogers asked.

"Not yet," answered Ben. "Someone has seen them just north of us. It won't be too much longer before they arrive."

"Our citizens have worked hard to make this the best butterfly stopover in the country," Mayor Rogers said. "I hope we don't have another festival like last year!"

What kind of a festival is there where you live?

28

The monarch butterfly migrates to Mexico each fall. Thousands of monarchs stop in Lakewood as they travel south. The town holds a huge festival every year to celebrate the butterflies' trip. Yet, last year's festival was different. Few monarchs had stopped.

At a town meeting, a scientist spoke to the people. "People are building houses, malls, and offices," said Professor Winglet. "The natural living space for butterflies has become smaller. So the numbers of butterflies have gotten smaller, too. The butterflies need trees to rest in. They need flowers to get nectar."

"What can we do to help?" someone asked.

"Lakewood can become a stopover again," Professor Winglet said. "Everyone can plant trees and flowers that appeal to butterflies."

Could your hometown be a butterfly stopover? Why or why not?

Immediately, the people in Lakewood began working together. The zoo built a special butterfly center. Visitors to the center could learn about butterflies. Children planted a butterfly garden at school. Other citizens planted special flowers in their yards. Liz and Ben were the official butterfly spotters.

"We have looked everywhere," said Ben. "The monarchs should be here by now."

Liz was also getting worried. The festival wouldn't be much fun if the butterflies did not arrive. Everyone would be disappointed. Yet there was a more serious problem. What would happen to the monarchs if their numbers were low again?

Liz and Ben were not giving up, though. The web site that tracked the butterflies' migration showed they should be in Lakewood very soon.

"We'll just have to keep looking," Ben said.

Say Something Technique
Take turns reading a section of text, covering it up, and then saying something about it to your partner. You may say any thought or idea that the text brings to your mind.

How has your school community worked together to solve a problem?

Ben and Liz walked back to the park. A group of children were practicing a dance for the festival. Some of the children wore flower costumes. They stood in rows and swayed from side to side as if they were blowing in the breeze. Other children wore monarch butterfly costumes. They danced in between the flowers.

Mrs. Chen, the dance teacher, clapped her hands.

"You make a beautiful butterfly garden, class!" Mrs. Chen said.

Mrs. Chen saw Liz and Ben. "Hello, official spotters! Have you seen any monarchs yet?" she asked.

Liz and Ben sadly shook their heads.

"We've looked all over," answered Ben. "I hope they are coming. Everyone worked so hard this year."

Have you ever been in a special program? What did you do?

Suddenly, a squeal came from one of the flower dancers. The other children began to giggle and dance around her.

"Ben! Liz!" Mrs. Chen shouted excitedly. "There is one garden you haven't looked in!"

Liz and Ben raced over. To their surprise, they saw a large monarch butterfly. It was sitting on the nectar snow cone cup that the little girl held.

"The butterfly must like the bright color of the costume and the smell of the nectar juice," said Mrs. Chen.

"One butterfly," said Liz. "It's a start!"

"It's more than a start," said Ben, pointing up to the sky.

What do you know about monarch butterflies or other creatures that migrate? Explain.

Everyone looked up. Thousands of butterflies were flying toward the garden.

"Hooray!" yelled Liz. "The monarchs are back!"

"And there are lots of them!" exclaimed Ben. "The festival can begin!"

32

Think and Respond

Reflect and Write

• You and your partner have read *The Great Butterfly Flutterby*. Discuss what you said to one another as you read.

• On one side of an index card, write a connection that helped you understand the story. On the other side, write how that connection helped you understand the story.

Initial Consonants in Context

Search through *The Great Butterfly Flutterby* to find words that begin with *b*, *d*, *f*, m, and *v*. Make a list of words with each initial consonant. Then compare your list with a partner's list.

Turn and Talk

MAKE CONNECTIONS

Discuss with a partner what you have learned about making connections when you read.

• How can making connections help you in your reading?

Look back at *The Great Butterfly Flutterby*. With a partner, discuss Liz and Ben's job as butterfly spotters. Talk about what would or would not make you a good butterfly spotter.

Critical Thinking

In a small group, brainstorm ways that a community can show it is a community. Then write a list of ways the community in *The Great Butterfly Flutterby* works together. Then answer these questions.

• How do you think town meetings help communities?

• What did you learn about communities from this story?

Contents

A Symphony of Whales

by STEVE SCHUCH   illustrated by PETER SYLVADA

Strategic Listening

Strategic listening means listening to ask "I wonder" questions. Listen to the focus questions your teacher will read to you.

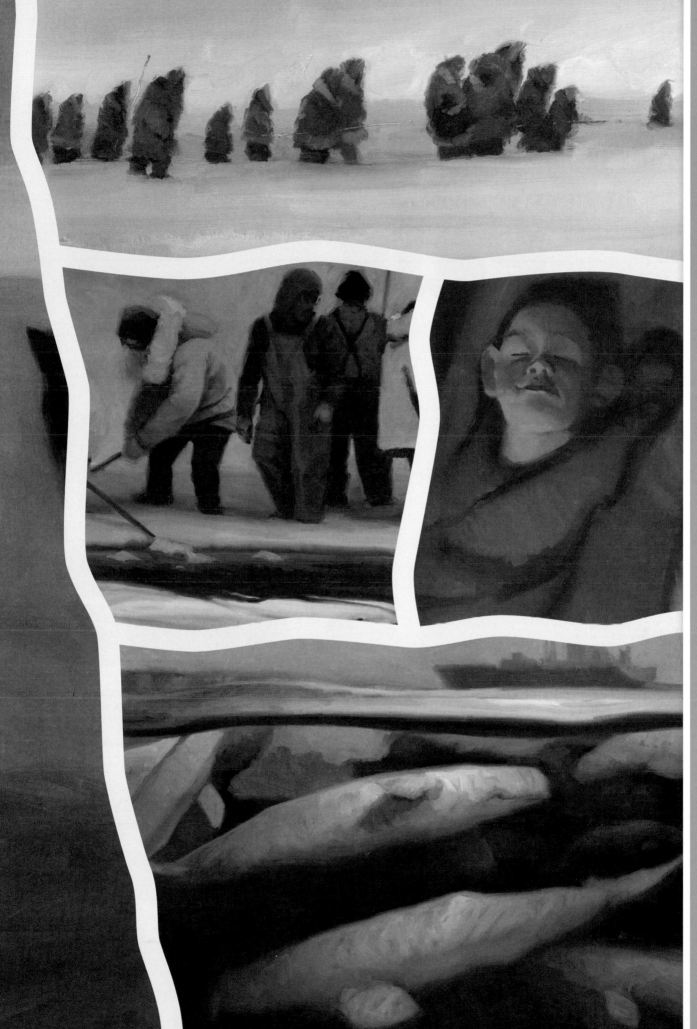

Postcard Pals

Dear Jake,

Hi! I'm your new pen pal. I live in New Mexico. You've probably never been here, so I'll tell you about it!

New Mexico has **landform** after landform. It has deserts, mountains, caves, and more. I like to **breathe** the dry desert air. We also have special **architecture**. Many buildings here are made out of clay. People have built houses like this for hundreds of years.

Please write back and tell me about your home!

Your friend,
Maria

Dear Maria,

Thanks for writing to me! I live in Healy, Alaska. It is near Denali National Park and Preserve. Denali has the highest **location** in North America. I know many people who work at the park. Every summer I wait **anxiously** for our backpacking trip into Denali National Park.

Write back soon!

Your friend,
Jake

Structured Vocabulary Discussion

When your teacher says a vocabulary word, you and your partner should each write on a piece of paper the first words you think of. When your teacher says, "Stop," exchange papers with your partner and explain to each other any of the words on your lists.

Throughout the week, add to your vocabulary journal entries. Record new insights and other words that relate to this week's vocabulary.

Picture It

Copy this chart into your vocabulary journal. Write an example in each space of a different **landform**.

landform		
mountain		

Copy this word web into your vocabulary journal. Fill in the word web with a **location** you would like to visit.

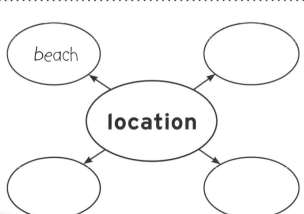

Ask Questions

WHAT does the text make you wonder about?

Think about the questions you have in your mind as you read.

TURN AND TALK Listen as your teacher reads from *A Symphony of Whales* and models how to ask questions. Then discuss with a partner answers to these questions.

• What did you wonder about as you listened?

• How do your questions help you understand the passage better?

TAKE IT WITH YOU When you ask questions, you let your curiosity help you become a better reader. As you read other selections, ask questions about words and ideas that are new or interesting to you. Use a chart like the one below to record your questions. Later, you can try to find the answers.

In the Text	"I Wonder" Question
"Each day, Glashka looked anxiously for a ship."	Does Glashka really believe a ship will come?
"But each day, a little more water turned to ice. Each day, the whales got weaker from hunger."	Are whales often trapped under ice in the ocean?

Meet the Music Man from New Orleans!

by Gus Conners

X
New Orleans

Does good music make you want to dance? If so, Wynton Marsalis will have you on your feet! Wynton is a jazz musician. He grew up in a musical family in New Orleans, Louisiana. Both jazz music and Wynton Marsalis were born in New Orleans! Many great musicians have come from New Orleans, and Wynton is one of the most famous.

Wynton was born on October 18, 1961. His father was a piano player and teacher. His mother was a singer. Some of his brothers were musicians, too. He got his first trumpet when he was six. Wynton practiced for hours. He was serious about studying music. By age seven, he was performing on stage.

Wynton Marsalis

As Wynton got older, he played more and more. At night he would go outside to play. Then, his family could get some sleep! He played in marching bands, jazz bands, and youth groups. At 14, he played with a famous New Orleans orchestra.

When Wynton was 17, he moved to New York City. He studied at a famous school of music. He drew crowds of people who came to see him play his trumpet. Two years later, he signed a contract to make records.

Today, Wynton is famous for writing and playing great jazz music. He has won many music awards. He also spends time teaching young people to play jazz. He travels to many places to share his music with others. He still considers New Orleans his home. In 2005, Hurricane Katrina flooded New Orleans. Since then, Wynton has helped raise millions of dollars to rebuild the city.

Wynton plays for a school.

43

Treats from Coast to Coast

Some foods are favorites across the country. You can probably find pizza dripping with sauce or grilled cheese sandwiches anywhere in the United States. But some of the best foods are special to certain states. What are some of these delicious dishes? Read these menus to find out!

Lobster

Missouri

- Toasted ravioli
- Barbecued chicken with mashed potatoes and gravy
- Frozen custard

Maine

- Clam chowder with crackers
- Lobster roll sandwich
- Steamed clams with drawn butter

Texas

- Chicken-fried steak with coleslaw and corn bread
- Baked potato with sour cream
- Barbecued brisket with corn on the cob

Toasted ravioli

Barbecued brisket

44

Consonant Blends

Activity One

About Consonant Blends

Consonant blends, such as *cr-*, *dr-*, *gr-*, *pr-*, and *-st,* are two or more consonant sounds that blend together but keep their own sounds. You may find a consonant blend at the beginning or end of a word. The following words have the consonant blends *cr-*, *dr-*, *gr-*, *pr-*, or *-st: creep, drain, group, price, test.* Listen for these consonant blends as your teacher reads *Treats from Coast to Coast.*

Consonant Blends in Context

Read *Treats from Coast to Coast* with a partner. Together, find words with consonant blends *cr-*, *dr-*, *gr-*, *pr-*, and *-st.* With your partner, practice saying each word aloud and listen for the blend.

Activity Two

Explore Words Together

With a partner, read aloud the words at right. Then circle all of the consonant blends. Make a list of new words that begin or end with the same consonant blends.

crash	growl
proud	draw
greedy	list

Activity Three

Explore Words in Writing

Write your own meal for a menu and use at least four words with consonant blends. Exchange your menu idea with a partner. Read your partner's menu idea and circle all of the consonant blends.

Country Mouse, City Mouse

A Classic Tale
retold by Nick Simser

*O*nce there was a mouse who lived in a red barn in the country. The mouse and his family ate corn that dropped from great stalks in the fields and green apples that fell from trees. They sipped water from a creek and slept on soft hay in the barn.

One day an invitation came in the mail. "Please come to City Mouse's party on Wednesday, next to the Sculpture Garden."

"You go," said his family. "And be sure to come back with stories for us."

"If you insist," said Country Mouse. "But I need a present to bring with me."

Country Mouse chose a beautiful pinecone that had fallen off a tree. He wrapped it in a maple leaf and tied it with hair from a horse's tail. On Wednesday, he hopped in Mrs. Brown's pocket because she was going to the city.

What questions do you have in your mind after you read this page?

INVITE

Soon Country Mouse arrived in the city. He cleaned his whiskers at a pond he found in a park.

"Eeeek, a *mouse*!" cried a woman. "We don't want mice in Loring Park!" A shiny red shoe was about to crush Country Mouse. He scampered off and landed in some mud. A bicycle barreled toward him and splashed him with water. Finally, he dashed under a banana peel.

After a little while Country Mouse started out again. He came to a wide street. Many people were hurrying to the other side. Soon Country Mouse caught a ride in the cuff of a businessman's pants. As the man passed the Sculpture Garden, Country Mouse jumped out.

"Thank you," he said.

What questions do you think Country Mouse might ask about life in the city?

Country Mouse knocked on a mouse-sized door in front of a big house.

"Ah, you must be Country Mouse," said City Mouse when he answered the door. "I can tell by the mud on your nose."

"That was because of the red shoe," Country Mouse started to say. But instead, he said, "Yes, it must have been from the farm."

"And I can tell by the water dripping off your ear," said City Mouse.

Country Mouse thought of the bicycle, but said, "Yes, it must have been from the farm."

"And you smell of bananas," said City Mouse.

"Yes, we like bananas on the farm," said Country Mouse.

Then he handed his gift to City Mouse. City Mouse noticed the maple leaf and horse hair.

"Interesting wrapping," he said. Then, remembering his manners, City Mouse added, "Interesting but charming. Thank you."

Reverse Think-Aloud Technique
Listen as your partner reads part of the text aloud. Choose a point in the text to stop your partner and ask what he or she is thinking about the text at that moment. Then switch roles with your partner.

What do you wonder about when Country Mouse meets City Mouse?

Country Mouse looked at the other gifts on a table. There was a jar with a gold top that said *Molly's Mud Pack for Shiny Mouse Fur*. There was a bottle with a silver cap that said *Natural Water for Good Mouse Health*. There was a bar of soap wrapped in a banana leaf that said *Soothe Your Senses with Our Finest Banana Soap*.

Country Mouse looked at his pinecone gift. The bow drooped. The maple leaf was torn. But the pinecone shone in the candlelight. It seemed to say, "I may not be popular, but I can be myself. That is enough."

So Country Mouse smoothed his fur and wiped the mud off his nose. *Stories*, he thought. *My family wants stories from the city. I'll not go home without them.* And he walked into the party.

What questions do you have about the gifts the other guests brought to the party?

Later that night, after he had returned home, Country Mouse told his family about the tall metal buildings he had seen. He told them that city people moved so fast that they looked like a blur.

"How strange," said the other mice.

"Yes," said Country Mouse. "But strangest of all is they don't like mud unless it is in a jar. They don't like water unless it is in a bottle. They don't like bananas unless they are in soap."

"Very odd," said the country mice.

"They do have nice manners, though," said Country Mouse. "And in that way, we are just alike."

Country Mouse grinned and snuggled into his soft hay bed, happy to be home again.

If you were in Country Mouse's family, what questions would you ask when Country Mouse returned home?

Think and Respond

Reflect and Write

- You and your partner have read *Country Mouse, City Mouse* and told what you were thinking. With your partner, discuss your thoughts.

- On one side of an index card, write down a question you or your partner had. On the other side, write down a possible answer.

Consonant Blends in Context

Search through *Country Mouse, City Mouse* to make a list of words you find with the consonant blends *cr-*, *dr-*, *gr-*, *pr-*, and *-st*. Then write 3 or 4 sentences that describe where you live. Use at least three words from your list.

Turn and Talk

ASK QUESTIONS

Discuss with a partner what you have learned so far about how to ask questions as you read.

- How can asking questions help you understand what you read?

Choose one of the questions you asked about *Country Mouse, City Mouse*. Discuss with a partner why you asked the question and how you found the answer.

Critical Thinking

In a small group, brainstorm the differences between living in the country and living in the city. Then answer these questions.

- How are the city and the country alike? How are they different?

- How is the place where you live similar to or different from the country or city?

A WORLD OF Holidays

The Dragon Boat Festival is a holiday celebration in China. People race long boats decorated with dragon heads. A favorite snack during the festival is rice dumplings. Many families take a long **voyage** on one of China's rivers to see a festival. Dragon boat racing is now an official sport in China and other countries.

Racing Dragon Boats in China

Holi is a colorful holiday in India. People take bright paint and splash it everywhere, even on each other! You can't **distinguish** one person from another. *Holi* celebrates the colors of spring. The festival is **popular** in cities and towns, from one **coast** to another in India. At the end of Holi, people wash off in a river or **creek** , or in bathtubs.

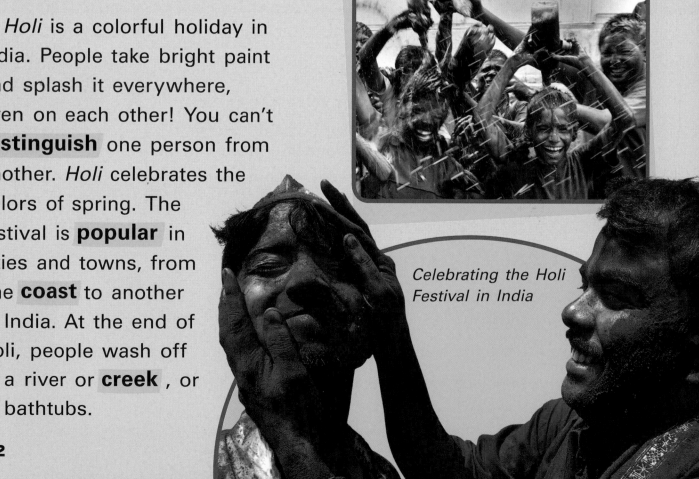

Celebrating the Holi Festival in India

Structured Vocabulary Discussion

When your teacher says a vocabulary word, take turns in a small group saying the first word you think of. When your teachers says, "Stop," the last person in the group that said a word explains how that word is related to the vocabulary word your teacher said.

Throughout the week, add to your vocabulary journal entries. Record new insights and other words that relate to this week's vocabulary.

Picture It

Copy this chart into your vocabulary journal. Fill in the boxes with things you might see, hear, smell, taste, or touch when visiting a **coast**.

coast	
see	gulls
hear	
smell	
taste	
touch	

Copy this word wheel into your vocabulary journal. Fill in the spaces with things you might take with you on a long **voyage**.

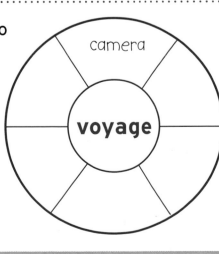

camera

voyage

The Erie Canal

folk song

Long ago, people often used boats to travel from place to place. In some places rivers did not connect centers of trade. So people built canals. A canal is a man-made river. A horse or mule walked beside the canal and pulled the boat. If the boat came to a low bridge, everyone had to watch out.

The Erie Canal was finished in 1825. It was built in New York. It helped people and goods travel from the east coast of the United States to areas as far away as Lake Erie. The Erie Canal was so useful that someone wrote a song about it.

A Traditional Folk Song

I've got a mule, her name is Sal,
Fifteen years on the Erie Canal.
She's a good old worker and a good old pal,
Fifteen years on the Erie Canal.
We've hauled some barges in our day,
Filled with lumber, coal, and hay,
And we know every inch of the way,
From Albany to Buffalo.

Chorus
Low bridge, everybody down!
Low bridge, for we're coming to a town!
And you'll always know your neighbor,
You'll always know your pal,
If you've ever navigated on the Erie Canal.

Welcome to
MINER TOWN!

Howdy! I'm Old Man Miner. Thanks for joining me on my tour of Miner Town. Back in its day, this was a rip-roarin' town! You see, in 1858 gold was discovered in the hills around town. A miner could move in, dip his pan in the stream, and pack his sack with gold. Overnight, Miner Town became a big and bold town. Stores, hotels, banks, and lots of fancy people came. The newspapers read, "Skip on Down! You Can Make a Fortune in Miner Town."

Then the mines dried up. People had no more gold to pay the way. Miner Town became a ghost town. Now all that is left are the spiders, flies, the stories, and me.

Miner Town Today

Miner Town, 1858

Word Families

Activity One

About Word Families

A word family is a group of words that have the same vowel and consonant ending and that rhyme. Here are examples of word families: *say, clay, fan, plan, tip, drip, cold, hold, lack, black, down,* and *clown.* When you change the consonant or consonant blend at the beginning of the word, you add to the word family. As your teacher reads *Welcome to Miner Town*, listen for the word families *-ay, -an, -ip, -old, -ack,* and *-own.*

Word Families in Context

With a partner, read *Welcome to Miner Town!* Find words that belong to the word families *-ay, -an, -ip, -old, -ack,* and *-own.* List the words you find that belong to each family.

Activity Two

Explore Words Together

With a partner, create a word family for each word on the right. Replace the beginning consonants of each word with other consonants. List the words that fit in each family.

pain	float
junk	snail
scrap	raw

Activity Three

Explore Words in Writing

Write a short rhyming poem about a place. Use as many words as you can from one word family. You may use one of the word families from Activity One or Two or make up a new family. Then have a partner find and underline all the words you used from that family.

How Ruby Came to the Farm

by Peter Hamilton as told to Ann Weil

Peter Hamilton lives on a farm in Queensland, Australia, with his family. Like many kids in the United States, he has a pet. His pet is no ordinary cat, dog, or bird, however. It is a kangaroo!

Queensland, Australia

One night Mum and I were driving in the outback under a full moon. We were on our way home when we saw a truck hit a kangaroo! Maybe the bright moonlight confused the roo. All of a sudden, it just hopped in front of the truck that was going too fast to stop in time.

What do you know about kangaroos? Where have you seen one?

Mum stopped the car and we helped the driver pull the dead roo off the road. It was sad, but I helped out. After the truck driver drove off, Mum grabbed a torch from the boot. She used the light to look for something along the side of the road.

Australian English

roo = kangaroo

torch = flashlight

boot = trunk of a car

outback = large desert area of Australia

I thought Mum was looking for a missing earring. It turned out she was looking for something else. She told me the dead kangaroo was a female. She could tell that it had had a baby recently. Mum thought that the joey might have been thrown clear in the accident.

After a few minutes I was ready to give up searching. But Mum could not leave with a joey freezing or starving to death out there. After several more minutes of searching, we found the little joey. It was alive!

Mum carefully placed the joey inside a clean sock. The baby roo was still pink, without any fur. I tucked the bundle under my shirt to keep the joey warm on her voyage to our home.

Have you ever rescued an animal, or seen an animal up close in the wild? Explain.

Australian English
joey = baby kangaroo

When we got closer to home, Mum had me call Wildlife Rescue. A ranger told me where we could get special milk for the joey. He warned us that kangaroos would get sick if we let them drink cow's milk.

For the next few days, Mum and I took turns wearing the joey under our clothes. If we couldn't do that, we put her in a sack and hung the sack in a warm part of the house. We used a liner that we could change like a baby's nappie.

Taking care of a joey is a lot of work. We had to give her four or five bottles of milk a day. Each feeding could take more than an hour! Soon, we took the joey to the vet for a checkup. The vet was pleased with how well the roo was doing. By then we had named her Ruby.

Two-Word Technique
Write down two words that reflect your thoughts about each page. Discuss them with your partner.

What kind of pets have you taken care of? Describe your activities.

Australian English
nappie = diaper

Ruby became part of our family. Her fur grew in. It was mostly the color of cream with a dark patch on her back. We watched her learn to crawl and then begin to hop. After a few months, Ruby could hop in and out of her cloth sack. She liked to explore and would sneak away on her own. Once I found her hopping on my bed. Another time she had crawled under the sink.

Everything was fine until one day Ruby crashed into a glass door in our house. She broke her tail. The vet said it would take time for it to heal. She had to stay in her sack. She couldn't hop around and play. Ruby didn't like that! I would catch her trying to sneak out. Someone had to watch her all the time. And her tail never did get completely well.

What television show or movie have you seen about a wild animal?

It is against the law in Australia to keep a wild animal as a pet. But, people can get permission to raise a joey that is all alone. The joey must be released back into the wild when it is old enough to live by itself. Ruby's broken tail would have made it hard for her to live on her own. That's why we got to keep Ruby on our farm!

People think Ruby is a wild kangaroo who wandered onto our farm. Nothing about the way Ruby looks is special enough to distinguish her from other kangaroos. People are gobsmacked when Ruby hops over to them. She only wants them to scratch her belly the way Mum and I always do!

Ruby is very different from wild kangaroos. She lives on a farm and not in the wild. And her family is not made up of kangaroos. Ruby's family is made up of people!

Do you know someone who takes care of wild animals? Explain what you know.

Australian English
gobsmacked = surprised

Think and Respond

Reflect and Write

- You and your partner have read *How Ruby Came to the Farm*. Discuss with your partner your words and thoughts.

- With a partner write a connection between the story and your experience. On one side of an index card, write the connection. On the other side write how the connection helped you understand the story.

Word Families in Context

Search through *How Ruby Came to the Farm* for *-ight* and *-atch* word families. List the words in each family. Then add more words to each family.

Turn and Talk

MAKE CONNECTIONS

Discuss with a partner what you have learned about how to make connections.

- How does making connections help you better understand your reading?

With a partner, discuss any pets you know about that are like Ruby. Share your connections with another partner team.

Critical Thinking

With a partner, brainstorm ideas about the life of a kangaroo in the wild. Discuss how Ruby's life changed after Peter and his mother adopted her. Then discuss answers to these questions.

- Is Ruby's life better in the outback or on the farm?

- Do you have any experiences with wild animals? If so, discuss how your experience is similar to or different from Peter's.

The Radiator Building at Night, 1927
Georgia O'Keeffe (1887–1986)

UNIT: *Thinking Like a* *Scientist*

THEME (3) What is Light?

THEME (4) How Does Electricity Work?

Viewing

This painting is of a building in New York City. When the artist painted the Radiator Building, it was only 3 years old. More than 80 years later, the building still stands. It is made of dark brick and is topped with gold. The gold top makes the building glow at night.

1. What do you see that is dark in the painting? What is light? Why are some parts shaded?

2. How does the artist show the different ways light can look?

3. What kind of electric light is shown in the painting?

4. What would this painting look like if there were no electricity?

In This UNIT

In this unit, you will learn about the properties of light and electricity. You will also discover how light and electricity work.

65

What Is Light?

Contents

Modeled Reading

Shared Reading

Interactive Reading

SNOWFLAKE BENTLEY

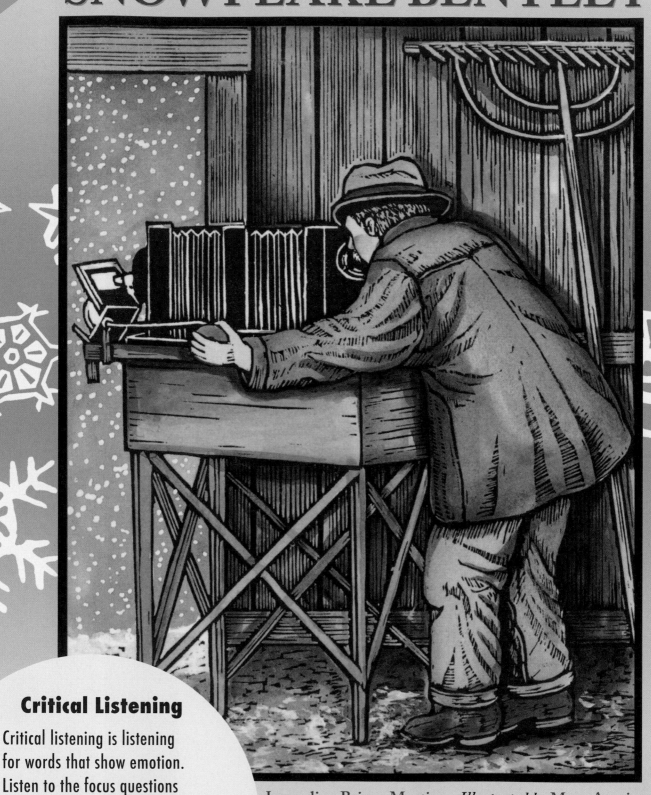

Critical Listening

Critical listening is listening for words that show emotion. Listen to the focus questions your teacher will read to you.

Jacqueline Briggs Martin   Illustrated *by* Mary Azarian

Come Join the
Winter Celebration

Lakeville's Winter Festival is about to begin. The fun starts Thursday at 5 P.M. with the Parade of Lights. Ride Lakeville's parade train straight to the Snowflake Dome!

A laser **beam projected** on the dome will bring snowflakes to life. See each **pattern** twirl into a different picture. **Monitor** snowflakes changing into snowmen, skiers, and stars. This year the show adds a new special effect, fog. The **absorption** of laser light makes colorful candles flicker and winter flowers bloom in the fog.

Structured Vocabulary Discussion

Read the words and phrases shown below. Pick one vocabulary word to go with each word or phrase. Share your answer with a partner and explain why you chose each word.

a guard watches people come and go

polka dots   *a movie on screen*

flashlight   *dark curtain on a window*

Throughout the week, add to your vocabulary journal entries. Record new insights and other words that relate to this week's vocabulary.

Picture It

Copy this word web into your vocabulary journal. Fill in the empty circles with things a person might **monitor**.

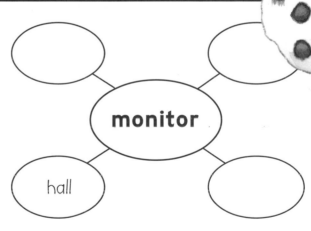

Copy this word chart into your vocabulary journal. Fill in each space with a type of **beam**.

beam
moon

Infer

When you **INFER**, you use your own ideas to help you understand what you read.

In the text **+** **In my head**

Combine what you read and what you already know.

TURN AND TALK Listen as your teacher reads from *Snowflake Bentley* and models how to infer. Then discuss answers to these questions.

- What knowledge did you use "in your head" while your teacher read aloud?

- How can inferring make you a better listener or reader?

TAKE IT WITH YOU Try to infer as you read other selections. Think about clues in the text and what you already know to better understand the story. Use a chart like the one below to help you.

In the Text		In My Head
"Day after stormy day he studied ice crystals. Their intricate patterns were even more beautiful than he had imagined."	+	Willie can *see* differences in the snowflakes. The microscope must help him *see* the patterns.

A Light in Our Tent

by Tonya Leslie

Antoinette and her sister Jocelyn were camping in the backyard. Antoinette had just closed the tent flap when Jocelyn said, "I don't like the dark." She held tightly to her stuffed bear. "Neither does Nico."

"You'll both be fine. Mom and Dad are in the house, just ten feet away," said Antoinette. "Besides, we have a flashlight and light from the full moon."

The girls snuggled into their sleeping bags. Antoinette read a book by flashlight while Jocelyn patted Nico's head.

"*Antoinette!*" Jocelyn cried after a few minutes of quiet. "Something is moving outside our tent! I'm scared!"

Antoinette pointed the flashlight at the tent flap. Just then, their dog stuck his fuzzy head inside. "Oh, it's just Pickle," said Antoinette, with a wave of her hand. "The moonlight cast Pickle's shadow on the tent. See? There's nothing scary at all."

Jocelyn lay quietly in her sleeping bag scratching the dog's ear. Antoinette listened to music. Suddenly Jocelyn cried, "ANTOINETTE! I see something flashing outside our tent!"

Antoinette crawled toward the door and slowly peeled back the flap. She saw the flash of light. She quickly put back the flap.

"Antoinette!" yelled Jocelyn. "Do you see that light? It's moving!"

"Yes, I see something. And I hear something too. It's right outside our tent!" whispered Antoinette.

The light stopped in front of their tent. The girls stared at the tent flap as a shadowy hand reached out to open it.

Suddenly, their mother poked through the tent flap with a tray of cookies and milk. She had a small lantern hanging from her wrist.

"It's just <u>Mom</u>!" said Jocelyn. "See? I told you there was nothing to be afraid of!"

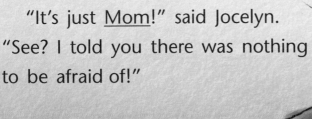

Fun with Silhouettes

A silhouette is a kind of picture. Some silhouettes are made from people's shadows. You can make one yourself!

What You Do

1. Tape a sheet of black construction paper to the wall.

2. Shine a light directly on the paper.

3. Seat your model between the paper and the light. Have your model turn to the side.

4. Check that the model's shadow is on the paper. To change the size of the shadow, move the model closer or farther away from the light.

5. Trace the shadow onto the paper. Use the white crayon or chalk.

6. Cut the paper on the line you traced. You made a silhouette!

What You Need

• a person as a model

• a lamp or flashlight

• black construction paper

• tape and scissors

• a white crayon or white chalk

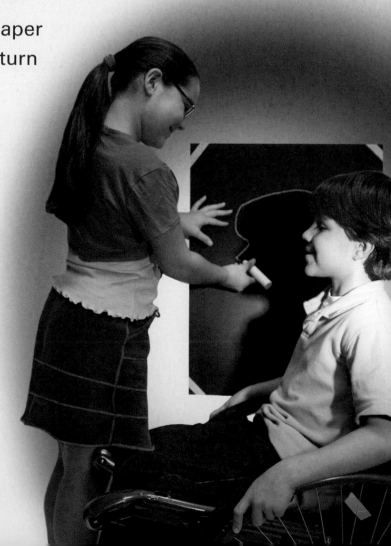

Long Vowels

Activity One

About Long Vowels

A vowel has the long sound when a consonant and *e* come after it. The *e* at the end of the word is silent. Here is a list of words with the long vowel sound: *bone*, *shade*, *huge*, *wise*, *these*, *prune*. As your teacher reads about making a silhouette, listen carefully for words with long vowel sounds.

Long Vowels in Context

In a small group, reread the text and make a list of words ending in a vowel, consonant, and silent e.

Activity Two

Explore Words Together

Work with a partner to change the words at the right to words with long vowel sounds. List all the new words you made. Be ready to share them with the class and explain how the vowel sound changes.

bit	kit
mad	plan
not	tub

Activity Three

Explore Words in Writing

Write a note to your partner using as many words as you can with the vowel/consonant/silent e pattern. Read each other's sentences and circle the words with this long vowel pattern.

Welcome to
Shadow Puppet
THEATER!

by Candyce Norvell

Imagine sitting in a quiet, dark room. Suddenly a big white screen is lit from behind. Music begins to play. Soon beautiful shadows take the shapes of monsters, animals, and people on the screen. This is shadow puppet theater.

A Bright History

Shadow puppets are different from the puppets you usually see. Shadow puppets are placed between a light and a screen. The screen must be thin enough to let light through. You see only the puppet's shadow through the screen.

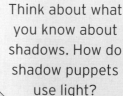

Think about what you know about shadows. How do shadow puppets use light?

Shadow puppets were made long ago in Asia. The people of different places, such as India, Java, and China, had different styles of puppets.

People used shadow puppets to tell stories. Often, the stories were tales of heroes.

The Shadow Puppet Theater of Java

In Java, people still love to watch shadow puppets. Java is part of the Asian country of Indonesia. The shadow puppets of Java show people with long arms and legs. Many puppets have cutout patterns that make beautiful shadows.

The theater is set up outdoors at night in a village. People gather to watch and listen. Bright lights help bring the moving, talking puppets to life.

The puppeteer does the voices of the puppets and sometimes sings. Another function of the puppeteer is to direct the music. Musicians play drums and other instruments. A shadow puppet play may last nine hours!

How hard do you think the puppeteer's job is?

Make Your Own!

You can put on shadow puppet shows for family and friends. Follow these steps to do it.

Reverse Think-Aloud Technique
Listen as your partner reads part of the text aloud. Choose a point in the text to stop your partner and ask what he or she is thinking about the text at that moment. Then switch roles with your partner.

What You Need

- scissors
- tissue paper
- lightweight cardboard
- stapler
- flashlight or lamp without a shade
- bamboo stick or straw
- tape or glue

1. Fold back two sides of a rectangular piece of cardboard so that it will stand up on a table. This will be the theater.

2. Ask an adult to help cut a large rectangular opening in the front of your theater. This is where the screen will go.

3. Cut sheets of tissue paper to be a little bigger than your frame. Stack 2–3 pieces of paper together and staple them to your frame. This makes the screen.

What kind of puppets will you make?

4. To create a puppet, cut whatever shape you like from cardboard. Tape a stick or straw to the shape so that it sticks out at least 3 inches below it.

5. Now put your theater on a table. Hold your puppet just behind the screen and shine a light behind it. The people on the other side of your screen should see the shadow of your puppet. Now you are ready to start the show!

With the light behind the puppet, where will the shadow fall?

Before the Show

There are two important things to remember. First, make sure your puppets are the right size for your screen. Second, turn out all the lights in the room except for the one you will use for your theater. This will help people see your puppets clearly.

Your show might be as simple as one puppet telling a joke. Or, you could use many puppets and different voices to tell a story. You might play music or demonstrate your talent as a singer. Let the show begin!

Why is it important to light the room the right way?

Think and Respond

Reflect and Write

- You and your partner took turns reading *Welcome to Shadow Puppet Theater!* Discuss the questions you asked, and the answers.

- On one side of an index card, write one idea that you can infer. On the other side, write down the text clues and your ideas that helped you make an inference.

Long Vowels in Context

Search through *Welcome to Shadow Puppet Theater!* to find words that end with a vowel, consonant, and silent e. List all the words you find and sort them by vowel sound.

Turn and Talk

INFER

Discuss with a partner what you have learned about how to infer.

- What does it mean to infer?

- How can you infer to understand what you read better?

Discuss with a partner the steps in putting on a shadow puppet theater. Write what you can infer about the puppeteers and their work.

Critical Thinking

Discuss with a partner any puppet shows that you have seen. Return to *Welcome to Shadow Puppet Theater!* Write down what you learned about a shadow puppet show. Then answer these questions.

- What story would you like to tell with shadow puppets?

- What puppet characters could you use to tell your story?

Camera Magic

Have you ever used a film camera, or wondered how it works?

A photograph is made when light hits film inside a film camera. The camera's shutter has a special **function**. It works like a door to let light in. When you snap a picture, the shutter opens and closes in less than a second. To **demonstrate**, close your eyes. Then open and close them quickly. This is how a shutter works! To take a picture at night, you can use a flash for light. A flashbulb contains a **filament**. The bulb lights up when you snap a photograph.

A camera has a special piece of glass in the front. This is the **lens**. The photographer adjusts the lens to **focus** the camera. Then, when the shutter opens, the image enters the camera and is burned onto the film.

Say, "Cheese!"

Structured Vocabulary Discussion

When your teacher says a vocabulary word, you and your partner should each write down the first words you think of on a piece of paper. When your teacher says, "Stop," trade papers and explain the words on your lists to one another.

Throughout the week, add to your vocabulary journal entries. Record new insights and other words that relate to this week's vocabulary.

Picture It

Copy the following word web into your vocabulary journal. Fill in the rectangles with names of things that have a **lens**.

microscope

lens

Copy the following word map into your vocabulary journal. Fill in the ovals with things people **demonstrate** for you. Fill in the boxes with things you can **demonstrate** for other people.

demonstrate

how to make a kite

How does the poet focus your attention on the way the shadow changes?

MY SHADOW

By Robert Louis Stevenson

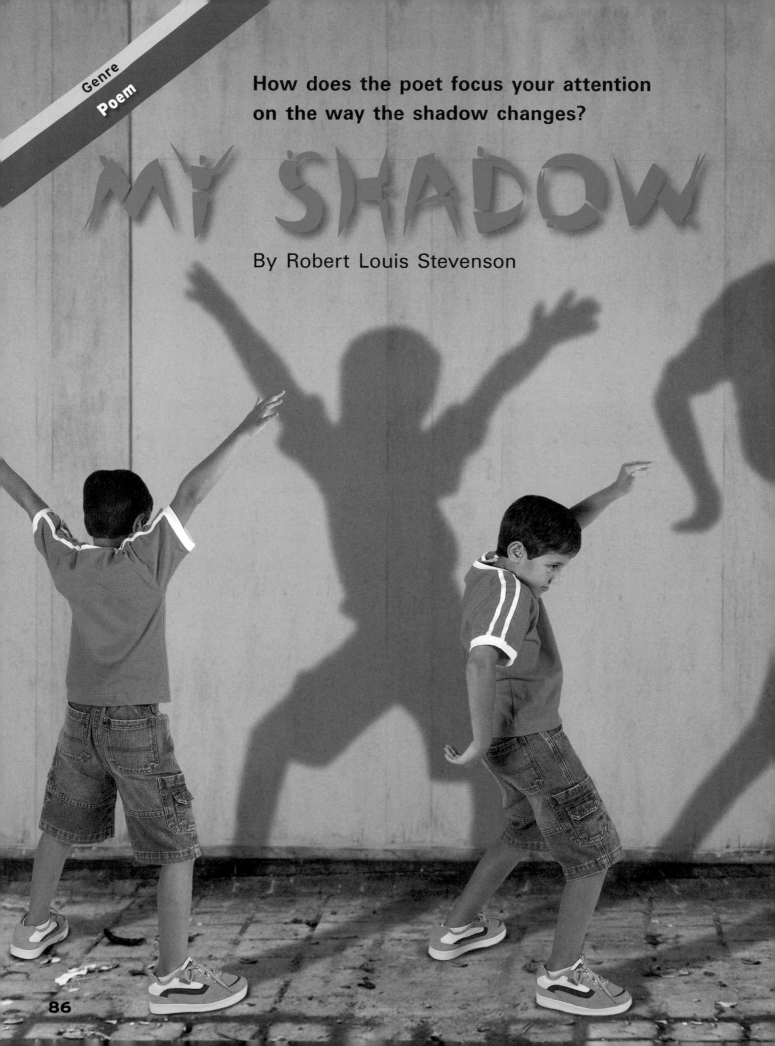

I have a little shadow that goes in and out with me.

And what can be the use of him is more than I can see.

He is very, very like me from the heels up to the head.

And I see him jump before me, when I jump into my bed.

The funniest thing about him is the way he likes to grow—

Not at all like proper children, which is always very slow;

For he sometimes shoots up taller, like an India-rubber ball,

And he sometimes gets so little that there's none of him at all.

How Are Rainbows Formed?

Coming live from KNN, the KIDS' NEWS NETWORK, I'm here with Professor Roy G. Biv. Let's have a colorful discussion about rainbows.

KNN: Professor Biv, we've all seen rainbows at one time or another. Can rainbows form at any time?

BIV: No, in order for a rainbow to form, rain must be falling in one part of the sky. The sun must also be shining from behind where you're looking.

KNN: Would you explain to our viewers how a rainbow is formed?

BIV: I'd be happy to. When sunlight enters a raindrop, the light waves bend and separate into different colored parts. Let me show you what I mean. This special piece of glass, called a "prism," shows how white light can separate into each color of the spectrum just like a rainbow.

KNN: Thanks, Professor Biv!

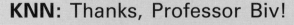

Words with *ch*, *sh*, *th*, *wh*

Activity One

About Words with *ch*, *sh*, *th*, *wh*

Some letter pairs, such as *ch*, *sh*, *th*, and *wh*, make a single sound. The words *change*, *ranch*, *shell*, *crash*, *thin*, *south*, *where*, and *whistle* are examples of words with these sounds. Listen for the *ch*, *sh*, *th*, and *wh* sounds as your teacher reads the interview.

Words with *ch*, *sh*, *th*, *wh* in Context

Reread the interview with a partner. Make a list of any words with the *ch*, *sh*, *th*, or *wh* sound that you find.

Activity Two

Explore Words Together

Look at the words to the right. With a partner take turns saying the words. Circle the *ch*, *sh*, *th*, or *wh* sounds in each word. Then think of new words with these letter pairs. Be ready to share your new words with the class.

chain	sharp
lunch	whale
mouth	thunder

Activity Three

Explore Words in Writing

Write a paragraph about what you might like to find at the end of a rainbow. Include several words that contain *ch*, *sh*, *th*, and *wh*. Then trade with a partner. Circle the *ch*, *sh*, *th*, or *wh* sounds in your friend's paragraph.

The Other Side of the Rainbow

By Annie Choi

Grandpa burst into the kitchen. "Evan, help me find a light bulb." He jerked open a cupboard and a mountain of dish towels fell on his head. "The light's out in the hallway. I guess the filament burned out. Let's go to the store."

"Can we stop at the flea market?" I asked.

"Sure," said Grandpa. "Let's go."

The flea market was packed with books, jewelry, clothes, and other things. While Grandpa hunted for light bulbs, I examined a table full of telescopes and binoculars. There was a strange glass lens unlike anything I had seen before.

What more would you like to know about Evan? What more would you like to know about his grandfather?

Carefully, I picked up the lens. It was smooth, clear, and fit in the palm of my hand.

"It's a prism."

I looked up and saw a man behind the table.

"What does it do?" I asked.

"Find a sunny spot and you'll figure it out. It's a bargain for fifty cents!" The man chuckled and smiled mysteriously.

What questions do you have about the prism?

I handed the man my change and shoved the prism in my pocket.

When I returned to my grandparents' house, I sprinted to the garden and took out my prism. I held it up to the sun and saw flashes of color dance and spin inside the glass. Then slowly, a rainbow stretched out in front of me. The rainbow arched brightly across the sky. It looked as if I could walk right on top of it.

Carefully, I stepped onto the rainbow. It wasn't just any rainbow—it was a bridge! But where did it go? I had to find out.

As I walked across the bridge, I saw a little town at the other end. I noticed something strange. Everything was in black and white. All the houses, streets, and cars were black and white. The sky, clouds, grass, and trees were all black and white. A black and white bee buzzed by.

I walked up to a small pond and looked at my reflection. I was still in color. I sighed in relief.

"Are you OK? You look a little . . . strange."

Standing next to me was a girl with black hair and glasses, which glowed against her white skin.

"I've never seen anyone like you before," the girl said. She blushed and her cheeks turned black. "My name is Mia."

Say Something Technique Take turns reading a selection of text, covering it up, and then saying something about it to your partner. You may say any thought or idea that the text brings to your mind.

How is the strange town like any other town? How is it different?

Mia reached over to touch my orange shirt. "What color is your shirt?"

"It's orange," I answered, "and my jeans are blue."

"I've never seen those colors before," she said quietly.

I took Mia to the rainbow bridge. Her eyes opened wide.

What questions can you ask to help you understand what's happening

"This is amazing," she gasped. "Our rainbows are only black and white."

Mia and I sat down on a black bench and chatted excitedly. Mia asked about the colors of different fruits. "In our town, apples are black!"

"Where I live, apples can be red, yellow, or green! Some are even a mix of colors!" I exclaimed.

"A mix?" Mia looked shocked.

The sun started to set. I noticed that the rainbow bridge was fading. I didn't want to go, but I didn't want to be stuck in this strange black and white town.

"I have to go," I said sadly, "but I'll come back. I'll bring you a surprise!" I thought about all the different colorful things I could bring back.

"Maybe I can visit you," Mia said hopefully.

When I got home, I showed Grandpa my prism. He grinned as he changed the light bulb in the hallway.

"I used to have one of those. It separates white light into all the colors of the rainbow. It's a neat little toy." He winked at me.

What "I wonder" questions could you ask about this page?

I smiled. "It's more than neat. It's special." I thought about Mia and the strange town. Maybe I could take Grandpa there the next time I visit my new friend.

Think and Respond

Reflect and Write

- You and your partner have read *The Other Side of the Rainbow*. Discuss the ideas that you got from the story.

- Think of a question related to one of your ideas. On one side of an index card, write the question. On the other side, write a possible answer.

Words with *ch, sh, th, wh* in Context

Search through *The Other Side of the Rainbow* to find words that have the *ch, sh, th,* and *wh* sounds. List the words by letter pairs. Then think of some new words with each sound.

Turn and Talk

ASK QUESTIONS

Discuss with a partner what you have learned so far about asking questions.

- How does asking questions help you understand what you read?

Choose one question you had when you read the text. Share your question with a partner and explain your answer.

Critical Thinking

In a small group, discuss what you know about how a real prism works. Return to *The Other Side of the Rainbow*. Write the ways the prism in the story is different from a real prism. Then answer these questions.

- Why is everything so different on the other side of the rainbow?

- Could Mia's world really exist?

Contents

Modeled Reading

Shared Reading

Interactive Reading

How Does Electricity Work?

Genre
Realistic Fiction

Thunder Cake

PATRICIA POLACCO

Appreciative Listening

Appreciative listening is listening for parts of the story that are funny or amusing. Listen to the focus questions your teacher will read to you.

Sparks are Flying

Have you ever heard a **crackling** sound in the sky and looked up to see lightning? You can see it indoors at the Theater of Electricity at the Museum of Science in Boston.

The museum is home to the Van de Graff generator. This machine is used to create lightning right before your eyes! If you want to learn about the **power** of lightning, come to the theater and see an amazing show.

When enough **electricity** has been made inside a dome of the Van de Graff, it releases an **automatic** spark, just like a storm cloud. This **glistening** bolt of electricity comes out of the machine. It looks like a lightning bolt in the sky.

Van de Graff Generator

Structured Vocabulary Discussion

Work in a small group. Classify the vocabulary words into two categories: words that name things and words that describe. When you're finished, share your ideas with the rest of the class. Be sure you can explain why each word belongs in its category.

Throughout the week, add to your vocabulary journal entries. Record new insights and other words that relate to this week's vocabulary.

Picture It

Copy this word wheel into your vocabulary journal. Fill in the top sections of the circle with toys that need **electricity** to work. Fill in the bottom sections with toys that do not need **electricity**.

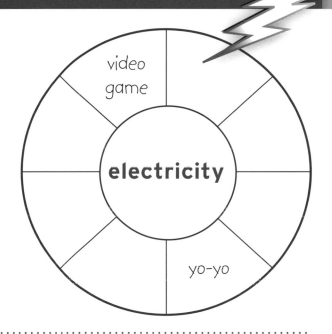

Copy this word web into your vocabulary journal. Fill in the empty circles with things that make **crackling** sounds.

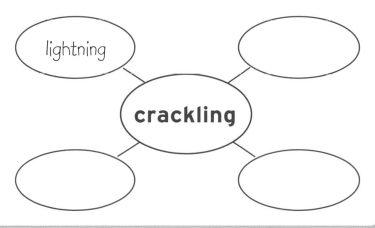

Synthesize

When you SYNTHESIZE, you bring ideas together.

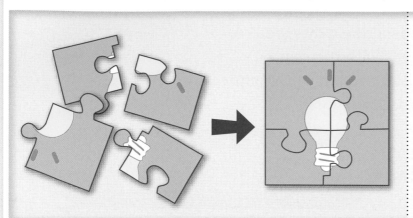

As you read, bring pieces of information together to form a new idea.

TURN AND TALK Listen as your teacher reads the following lines from *Thunder Cake* and models synthesizing. Then discuss answers to these questions.

• Why does the girl say she is not brave?

• What does her grandmother say about the girl?

• Is the young girl still afraid of storms? Explain.

TAKE IT WITH YOU When you synthesize ideas, you put together different pieces of information. These pieces create a pattern that makes a new idea. Use a chart like the one below to help you synthesize your ideas.

After Reading I Know That...

The girl thinks she is not brave.

The girl gets eggs and milk.

The girl goes to the dry shed through the Tangleweed woods. She climbs the trellis.

This Information Helps Me Understand That...

The girl was able to get over her fears by staying busy.

Franklin's Spark

by Chris Bennett

Have you ever wondered how lightning gets its power? Back in 1752, so did Ben Franklin. And like a good scientist, he set out to find out the answer.

Hypothesis

Franklin wanted to prove that lightning is an electric force in nature. This was his hypothesis. A hypothesis is an idea that you test to see if it is true.

Experiment

Franklin did an experiment to test his idea. He attached a pointed wire at the end of a strong kite. At his end of the kite string, he attached a key. Franklin and his son flew the kite on a stormy day. Franklin saw the hairs on the kite string stand on end and separate from each other. This was the sign of an electric force. A spark jumped from the key to his finger.

Conclusion

When Franklin saw the spark, he knew that a charge of electricity had moved down the wet kite string to the key. Franklin concluded that lightning carried electricity in it.

Results

Franklin shared his results with others. His experiments helped people to understand the science of electricity.

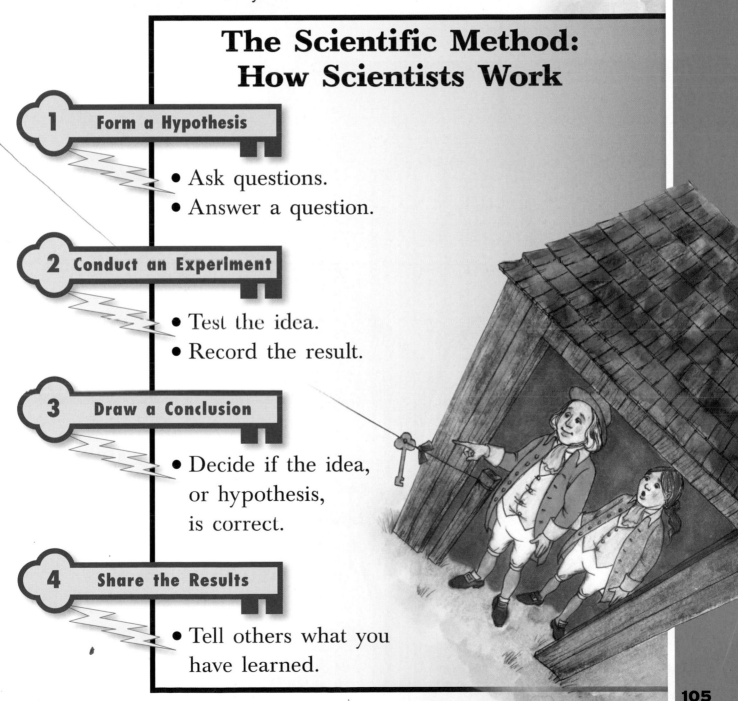

The Scientific Method: How Scientists Work

1 Form a Hypothesis

- Ask questions.
- Answer a question.

2 Conduct an Experiment

- Test the idea.
- Record the result.

3 Draw a Conclusion

- Decide if the idea, or hypothesis, is correct.

4 Share the Results

- Tell others what you have learned.

Word Study

Static Electricity

Do you know why you can shock someone after walking across a carpet in your socks? The "shocking" answer is static electricity!

neutron

proton

electron

Static electricity starts with tiny particles called atoms. In an atom, electrons have a negative charge. Protons have a positive charge. Neutrons have no charge.

You may walk across a carpet and touch a doorknob. ZAP! You get a shock. Your feet pulled electrons from the carpet. But electrons always want to get back together in orbit with protons. So they "leap" to the doorknob when you touch it. This can give you a painful shock!

Words with *ai, ay, ea, ee*

Activity One

About Words with *ai, ay, ea, ee*

When two vowels come together, the first vowel often has the long vowel sound. The second vowel is silent. Here are some words with the long vowel sounds *ai, ay, ea,* and *ee*: *mail, raise, hay, stay, team, peach, bee, meet.* As your teacher reads *Static Electricity,* listen carefully for these sounds.

Words with *ai, ay, ea, ee* in Context

Read *Static Electricity* again with a partner. Find words that have the long *a* sound spelled *ai* or *ay* and the long *e* sound spelled *ea* or *ee*. Write the words for each vowel sound you find in a separate list.

Activity Two

Explore Words Together

Work with a small group to list other words that have the same *ai, ay, ae, ee* long vowel sounds as the words listed at the right. Challenge each other to come up with as many words as you can. Be ready to share your group's lists of words with the whole class.

tail	spray
seal	tea
cheek	train

Activity Three

Explore Words in Writing

Write sentences telling how you feel about lightning. Use words from the activities above. Share your sentences with a partner. Find and circle all the words in each other's sentences with long vowels spelled *ai, ay, ea,* and *ee*.

Electrified!

by Kathleen Ermitage

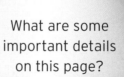

Last season, Alex didn't score a goal—not one measly goal. "Today is going to be different," Alex told himself. "Today, I'm going to be the hero."

Carlos kicked the ball to Alex. Just then a bolt of lightning shot down from a big, black cloud.

"Stop the game!" the referee called out. "We can't stay here. Everyone to the field house. Now!"

Lightning streaked across the sky. Rain poured down in sheets. Both teams and their fans ran for shelter.

"Alex, your hair is standing straight up!" his mother said when they were inside. "Are you OK?"

"My head feels a little tingly," he said.

"Hey, what's with your hair?" asked Jamal.

"My hair feels like wires. And now my hands feel tingly, too," Alex said.

> What are some important details on this page?

The lights inside flickered off. Alex spun around and raised his hands to his head. There was a loud ZZZZap. Suddenly, the power was back on! Everyone stared at Alex. His dark hair was bright yellow, and his fingers glowed. Thin lightning bolts flashed from his fingertips.

"I don't know what just happened, but that was amazing!" said his dad. "I think you made the power go on. You're electrified!"

The storm passed, and it was safe for everybody to leave.

On the way home, Alex stared at his hands and practiced throwing some bolts at his wet shoes. In seconds, the shoes dried as if he had set them near an electric heater.

What clues show Alex is electrified?

At home, Alex wondered what to do next with his new powers. His dad ordered a pizza. When the pizza arrived, Alex opened the box and suddenly had an idea.

I like the cheese to be brown on top. I wonder if I . . . Alex thought. He rubbed his head and raised his hands up in the air. He aimed for the pizza and bolts of electricity flowed from his fingers.

ZZZZap. Pow! The cheese sizzled and browned and turned gooey.

"Yum. That's just the way I like it!" said Alex.

Alex's mom and dad stared at each other. Outside, the lightning and thunder had started again.

Two-Word Technique Write down two words that reflect your thoughts about each page. Discuss them with your partner.

How would you describe Alex's new power?

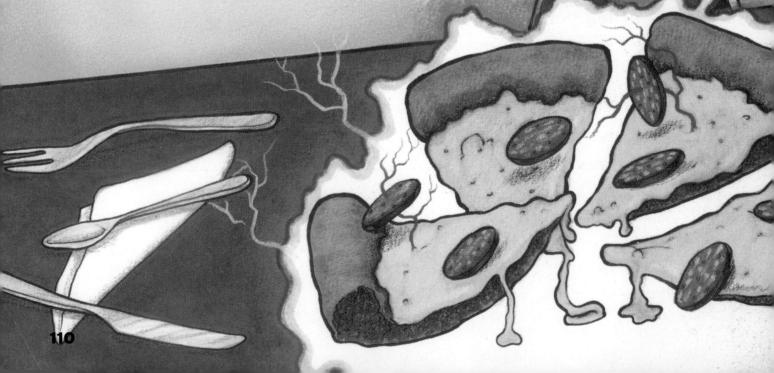

110

"The weather station should have information about the storm," said Alex's dad as he turned on the TV.

Then suddenly the TV blinked off and all the lights went out.

Alex wiped off his greasy hands. He touched his tingly head and waved his hands over the circuit in the back of the TV. ZZZZap. Pow! Power on!

He continued to wave his hands. All of the lights went on, and each appliance began to whir. Power on! His hair flashed a bright yellow again.

Alex was proud of his new power. He tied his sweatshirt around his shoulders like a cape.

Alex saw that the street outside was dark and silent. No one had electrical power.

He and his dad visited every house in the neighborhood. ZZZZap. Pow! Power on!

What kind of activities is Alex able to do with his new power?

Then, Alex found a frightened kitten high up in a tree. He pointed at the branch it clung to. ZZZZAP! The branch snapped. Alex caught the kitten.

"Hooray!" Brenda, their neighbor yelled. She ran across her yard to Alex.

"How did you do that?"

Alex smiled and winked at his dad. He straightened his cape.

When Alex and his dad reached home, the rain, lightning, and thunder stopped. The storm had finally passed.

"Hey Dad, the tingling on my head is gone. I think my power is fading," Alex said. His dad stepped closer to look at the top of Alex's head.

What information in the story helps you decide that Alex is a hero?

"Well, I guess even you can run out of power," his dad said.

"Let's check the weather report. Maybe there's another storm coming," Alex said with a twinkle in his eye.

Think and Respond

Reflect and Write

- You and your partner have read parts of *Electrified!* and written two words for each page. Discuss the words.

- On one side of an index card, write two details from the story. On the other side of the index card, write a new idea you had based on these details.

Words with *ai*, *ay*, *ea*, *ee* in Context

Search through *Electrified!* and list all the words you find spelled with *ai*, *ay*, *ea*, and *ee*. Then circle the words that have the long *a* or long *e* sound.

Turn and Talk

SYNTHESIZE

Discuss with a partner what you have learned so far about how to synthesize.

- How do you synthesize information as you read?

With a partner, reread page 111. Discuss how the details on this page help you make a statement about Alex.

Critical Thinking

With a partner, discuss what you know about electricity. Return to the story and make a list of the ways Alex uses electric power. Then answer these questions.

- How did Alex become electrified?

- Which parts of the story could happen? Which parts could not?

Unplugged

Have you ever had the electricity go out in your home or school? On August 14, 2003, this happened to more than 50 million people in the United States and Canada. People could not ride the subway, use their office computers, or use any home **appliance**. When electrical power fails over a large area it is called a blackout. A blackout reminds people of the **benefits** of electricity.

Too Much Power Means No Power

Blackouts happen when there is too much electricity for power lines to carry. Too much electricity for the power lines can cause an electric **circuit** to shut down. When a circuit shuts down, electric current cannot **advance** along the power lines. When there are not **alternative** power lines for the current, electricity builds up. Then, a blackout happens!

In 2003, New York City was blacked out for more than a day.

Structured Vocabulary Discussion

Work in a small group. When your teacher says a vocabulary word, take turns saying the first word you think of. Be ready to explain why your word is related to the vocabulary word.

Throughout the week, add to your vocabulary journal entries. Record new insights and other words that relate to this week's vocabulary.

Picture It

Copy this word web into your vocabulary journal. Fill in each circle with the name of an **appliance** that uses electricity.

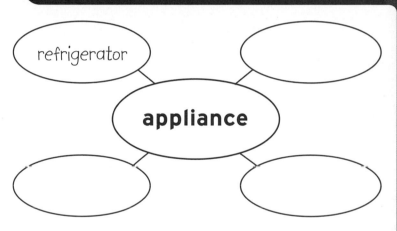

Copy this word wheel into your vocabulary journal. Give examples of the **benefits** of electricity.

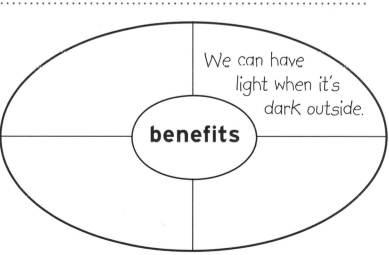

Electricity Haikus

by Lorraine Sintetos

From a hill, I watch
evening advance on the town—
lights blanket below.

I'm falling asleep.
The night light casts a soft glow.
The radio plays.

There's crashing thunder.
Clouds collide—fizzle and spark—
lightning splits the sky.

Overhead I hear
buzz, whine, roar, sizzle. Wires sing,
"Whee! Electricity's free!"

Outside in the night
power lines sag in the wind,
don't give up the fight.

Electricity
by nature or by man, has
power to command.

CHICAGO'S Wrigley Field

August 9, 1988

Hi Nate,

You won't believe what I did last night. I got to go to the first night game at Wrigley Field! Wrigley was built in 1914. Back then, stadiums didn't have the big electric lights that they all have today. Here in Chicago, fans wanted to keep things like the old days.

Our seats were just a few rows from the field! When the lights came on, everyone cheered. It started with a low glow. Then the lights got brighter. It seemed funny cheering on thousands of light bulbs.

Soon after the game began, it started raining. We tried to keep dry, but we got soaked going home. We could have used a boat instead of our car. Come and visit soon! We'll go see a night game at Wrigley Field.

Your friend,

Joanie

Wrigley Field
1060 W. Addison Street
Chicago, IL 60613

NATE CHURNEY

1324 WEST MAPL

MARIETTA, GA

Words with *ie*, *igh*, *oa*, *ow*

Activity One

About Words with *ie*, *igh*, *oa*, *ow*

When you see *oa* or *ow* together in words, they often make the long *o* sound. Here are some examples: *toad*, *throat*, *goal*, *show*, *tow*, *blow*. You hear the long *i* sound when *ie* and *igh* appear in words such as *tie* and *might*. As your teacher reads *Chicago's Wrigley Field*, listen for the long *ie*, *igh*, *oa*, and *ow* sounds.

Words with *ie*, *igh*, *oa*, *ow* in Context

Read *Chicago's Wrigley Field*. Make a list of all the *ie*, *igh*, *oa*, and *ow* words you find. Compare your list with a partner's and read the words out loud to each other.

Activity Two

Explore Words Together

flow	load
mow	soap
pie	sight

Team up with two other partners. Together, write sentences using at least two of the words in the box in each sentence. Read your sentences out loud to the other teams.

Activity Three

Explore Words in Writing

Use the words from the previous activity and any new ones with the *ie*, *igh*, *oa*, and *ow* sounds. Write a postcard to a friend. Exchange postcards with a partner and read them out loud to each other.

STREET

30064

Power Posters

by Arthur Nash

May 9, 5:00 P.M.

I am an artist hired to make posters for a show about new and better ways to make electricity. But I have to find out more. So this week I'm visiting some places where they are using new forms of electricity.

> Who might have hired the artist to make posters about new forms of electricity?

May 10, 1:35 P.M.

I'm on an airplane heading to Florida—the Sunshine State—to see how people make things run on sunlight.

My posters will be in a show about cleaner ways to produce electricity—cleaner than burning coal, gas, and oil. Less pollution is only one of the benefits of alternative ways to make electricity. Some of these new ways will cost less, too.

I start to draw on my sketchpad, but the roar of the plane is too loud for me to work. I wish this were a quiet plane powered by the sun's light.

May 11, 3:30 P.M.

Today, a man named Jack drove me around the Solar Center. Jack's solar car looked like a flying saucer. "It's not as big as a car," Jack said. "But at least we won't have to stop for gas."

We passed fields of solar panels. The panels use sunlight to make electricity. Solar energy can heat, light, and even cool people's homes. The Solar Center's job is to show people how easily the sun can work for them. Using solar energy can save money and help the environment too!

May 11, 6:30 P.M.

Jack will take me for a ride in a solar boat tomorrow. We will see water in a different way at the top of the Hoover Dam.

> Why do you think the artist will be visiting the Hoover Dam next?

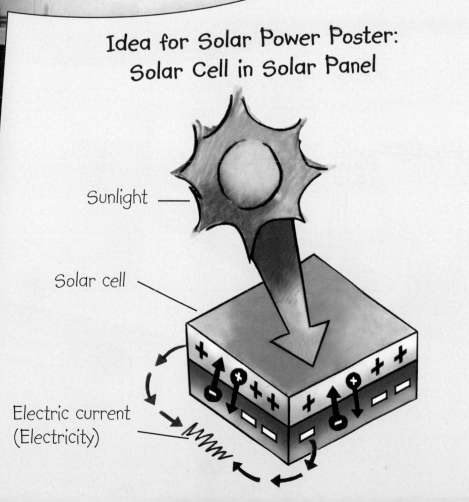

Idea for Solar Power Poster:
Solar Cell in Solar Panel

Sunlight

Solar cell

Electric current
(Electricity)

May 12, 4 P.M.

I'm here at the Hoover Dam on the Colorado River. My second poster will be about water power. The dam changes the natural flow of the river. As water enters the dam, turbine engines (machines) turn the energy of moving water into electricity. Electricity from the Hoover Dam lights up the city of Las Vegas! There is very little pollution at Hoover Dam.

Partner Jigsaw Technique
Read a section of the journal with a partner and write down one inference. Be prepared to summarize your section and share one inference.

Do you think that building the Hoover Dam was a good idea? Why?

May 13, 7:15 A.M.

My next stop is California. I'm going to see a new way to use wind power to make electricity: flying windmills. These windmills use the strong, steady winds high in the sky to create energy.

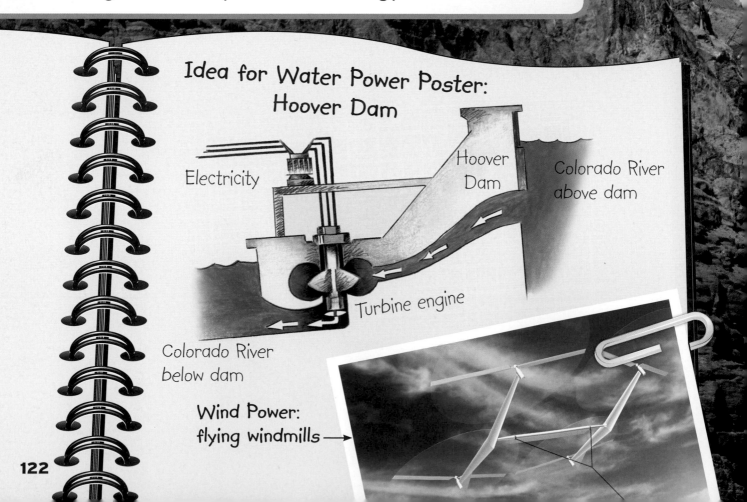

Idea for Water Power Poster: Hoover Dam

Electricity

Hoover Dam

Colorado River above dam

Turbine engine

Colorado River below dam

Wind Power: flying windmills →

122

May 13, 4:50 P.M.

These flying windmills are shaped like the letter *H*. A blade at each end of the *H* spins when the wind blows it. Wind energy is changed into electricity. The electricity goes down to the ground through a cable. The cable also keeps the flying windmill from blowing away.

Why might a flying windmill be a cheaper way to produce electricity?

May 13, 7:10 P.M.

I was running out of energy myself. Time to eat! While waiting at a diner, I read about some college students. They drove across the country in a bus that ran on vegetable oil! They stopped at fast-food restaurants instead of gas stations. The students put used cooking oil in the fuel tank. The bus ran fine. It smelled like fried food!

May 14, 11:15 A.M.

Using the energy from something like vegetable oil is cleaner than burning gas. This is true for cars and buses. It is also true for power plants.

I'm at a power plant that burns materials such as wood, corn stalks, and some grasses. Burning these materials makes electricity. The power plant burns waste in a furnace from mills and farms. This is cleaner and cheaper than burning coal.

I now have what I need to paint the posters. I also have a new way of thinking about electricity.

Which alternative source of electricity do you think is the best? Why?

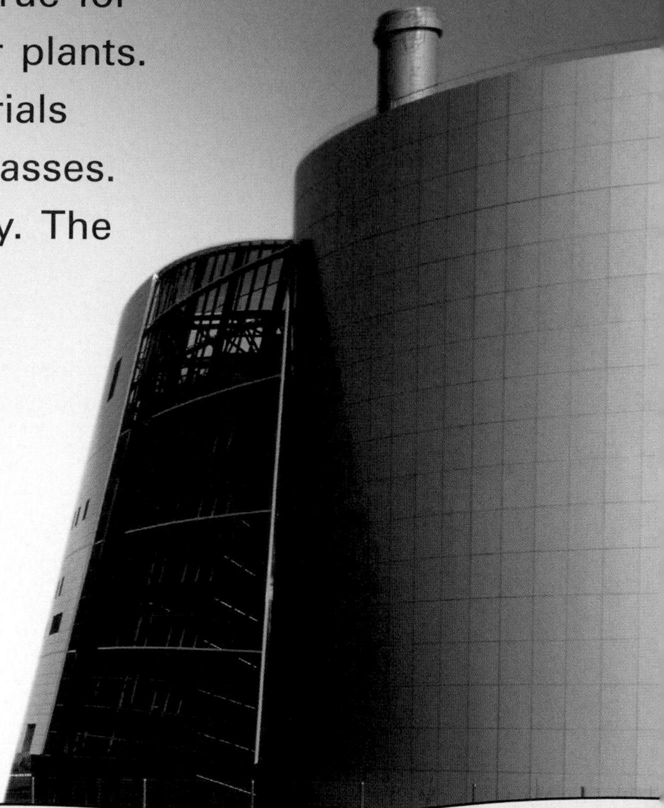

Idea for Vegetable Power Poster: Power Plant

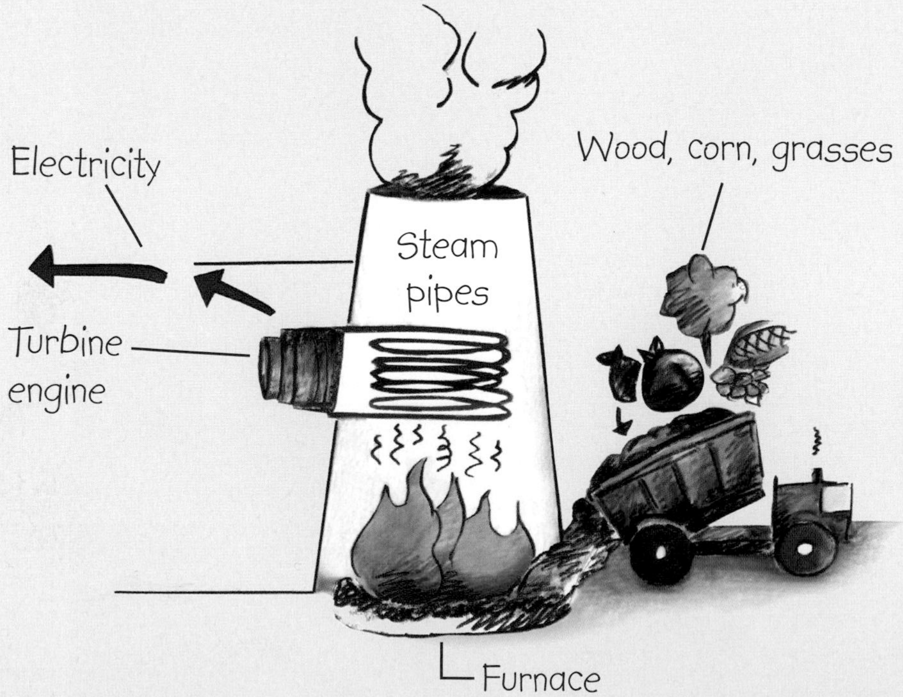

Electricity

Turbine engine

Steam pipes

Wood, corn, grasses

Furnace

124

Think and Respond

Reflect and Write

- You and your partner read sections of *Power Posters* and made inferences. Discuss your inferences.

- On one side of an index card, write an inference you can make about energy choices. On the other side, write the clues in the text and your own experience that helped you make the inference. Share your inferences with another partner team.

Words with *ie*, *igh*, *oa*, *ow* in Context

Search through *Power Posters* and list all the words you find spelled with *ie*, *igh*, *oa* and *ow*. Then exchange your list with a partner to see if either of you missed any.

Turn and Talk

INFER

Discuss with a partner what you have learned so far about how to infer.

- How can making inferences help you read beyond what the author wrote?

Choose one inference you made while reading *Power Posters*. Discuss your inference with a partner.

Critical Thinking

Talk with a partner about the alternative sources of electricity described in the journal. Choose one alternative source and write why you think it is a good idea. Then answer these questions.

- Why is it important to generate electricity?

- Why is it important to find new ways of generating electricity?

Central Park, 1914–15
Maurice Prendergast (1858–1924)

UNIT:

Then and *Now*

THEME **5** **Times Have Changed**

THEME **6** **Roads to Travel On**

Viewing

The artist painted this artwork almost a hundred years ago. He often painted city scenes with people. Central Park is still in the middle of New York City. Public roads still allow people to pass through the park.

1. What details from the painting show you that this was painted more than one hundred years ago?

2. If an artist painted Central Park today, how might the painting be similar to and different from this one?

3. How do you think most people traveled around at the time of this painting?

4. What kinds of transportation that you might see today are not in the painting?

In This UNIT

In this unit, you will read about how people lived in the past. You will also read about the different types of transportation that people have used over time.

Contents

Genre

Expository

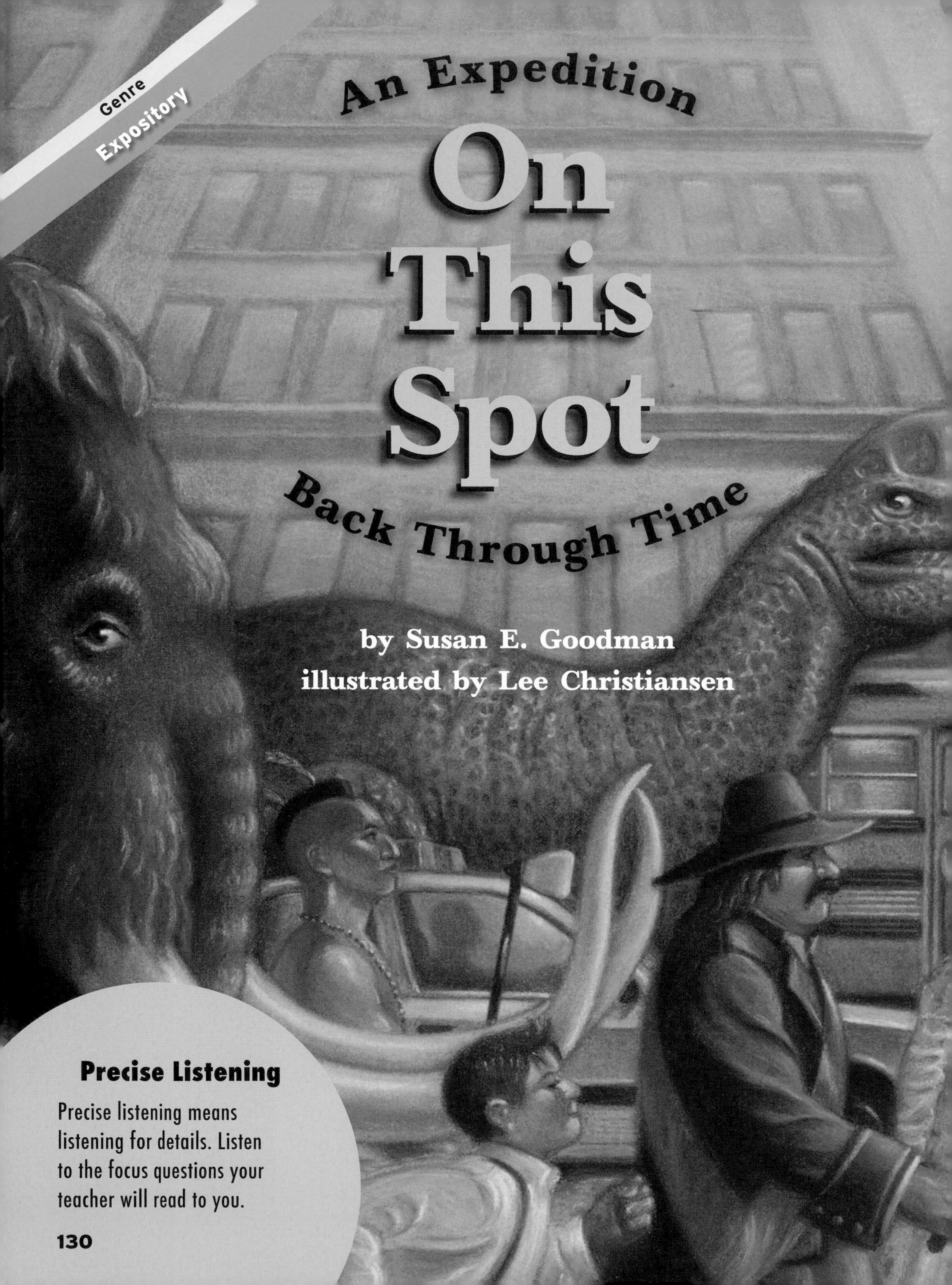

An Expedition On This Spot Back Through Time

by Susan E. Goodman

illustrated by Lee Christiansen

Precise Listening

Precise listening means listening for details. Listen to the focus questions your teacher will read to you.

FIREFIGHTERS
THEN AND NOW

New York City firefighters have changed a lot. Here are a few ways.

Then: 1600s The Rattle Watch was the city's first fire department. It helped keep the growing **settlement** safe. Each man had a **territory**. When a fire broke out, he sounded his rattle. People from **neighboring** places came to help. They made two lines. One line passed buckets of water to the fire in a "bucket brigade." The other line passed the empty buckets back.

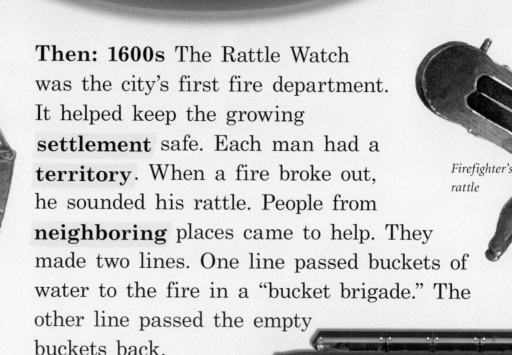

Firefighter's rattle

Firefighter in 1600s

Now: 2000s Today, computers sound the fire alarms at the fire station. Firefighters race to fires in trucks that carry 500 gallons of water. A pump forces water out of long hoses. Some firefighters also speak two **languages**. This helps them work with the **diversity** of people in the city.

Firefighter in 2000s

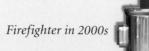

Structured Vocabulary Discussion

Work with a partner or in a small group to fill in the following blanks with vocabulary words. Discuss your answers with the class.

Alike is to *same* as *difference* is to _____.

Far is to *near* as *distant* is to _____.

Village is to _____ as *area* is to _____.

> *Throughout the week, add to your vocabulary journal entries. Record new insights and other words that relate to this week's vocabulary.*

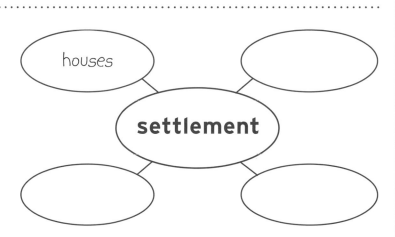

Picture It

Copy this chart into your vocabulary journal.
Fill in the blanks to tell about the times you have seen other **languages** written and heard other **languages** spoken.

languages **written**	languages **spoken**
letter from my grandma	my house

Copy this word organizer into your vocabulary journal. Fill in the empty circles with things you might see in a **settlement**.

houses

settlement

Monitor Understanding

CHECK to make sure you are UNDERSTANDING what you read.

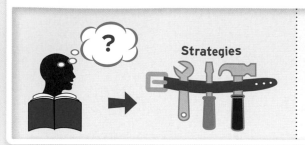

Strategies

Check your understanding. When you don't understand, try a few key strategies to help.

TURN AND TALK Listen as your teacher reads from *On This Spot* and models how to monitor understanding. Then with a partner discuss answers to these questions.

• Is there any part of the text that I don't understand?

• What can I do to help myself understand better?

TAKE IT WITH YOU Monitoring your understanding is a way to check how you are reading. Stop yourself as you read and make sure you understand what you have read. If a part is unclear, use a strategy to help you figure out what it means. Use a chart like the one below to help you monitor understanding.

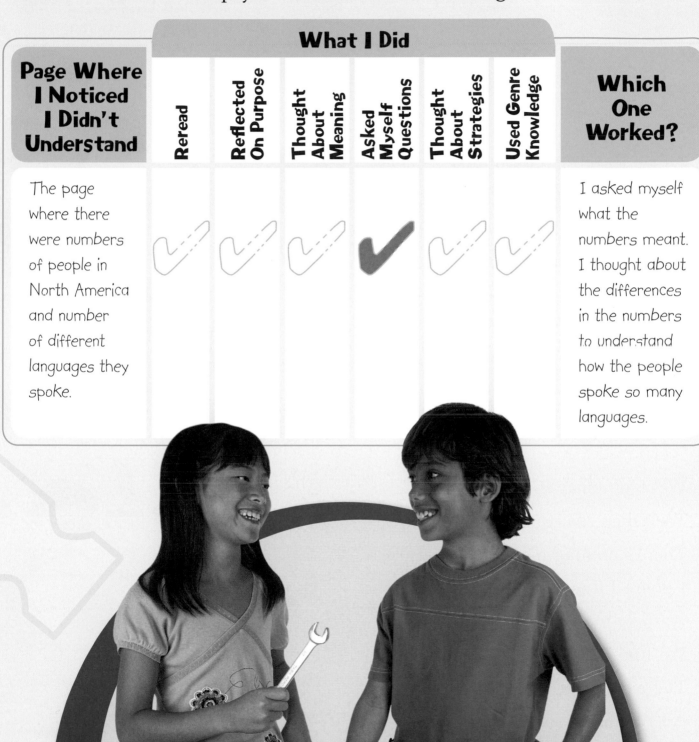

Page Where I Noticed I Didn't Understand	What I Did						Which One Worked?
	Reread	Reflected On Purpose	Thought About Meaning	Asked Myself Questions	Thought About Strategies	Used Genre Knowledge	
The page where there were numbers of people in North America and number of different languages they spoke.	✓	✓	✓	✔	✓	✓	I asked myself what the numbers meant. I thought about the differences in the numbers to understand how the people spoke so many languages.

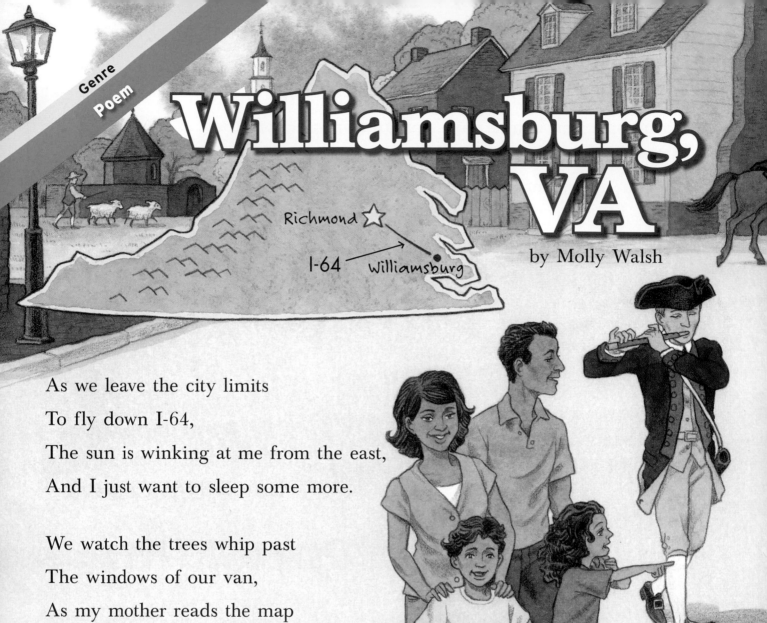

Williamsburg, VA

by Molly Walsh

As we leave the city limits
To fly down I-64,
The sun is winking at me from the east,
And I just want to sleep some more.

We watch the trees whip past
The windows of our van,
As my mother reads the map
And tells us of the plan.

We're on our way down south,
To Williamsburg, VA.
There's nothing modern in that place.
I doubt I'll want to stay.

We find the town. It's trapped in time—
The eighteenth century.
All the buildings and the people
Are living history.

The call of fifes and drums
Greets us as we begin our day.
The pounding drums...the marching feet...
It's a Colonial play!

Then girls wearing long skirts and hats
Roll hoops down Prince George St.
We hear the blacksmith's anvil sing.
New shoes for the horse. What a treat!

We buy hand-made soap and candles,
A few quills, ink, and wax.
Instead of a modern e-mail, I'll send
An old-fashioned letter to Uncle Max.

By day's end, I'm stuffed with tasty food.
We've learned to curtsy and to bow.
A Colonial village is like night to my day,
But I'd like to return again—somehow!

What Was Once New

What technology do you see around your house and school? Do you see cell phones? How about computers? Video games? Have you ever wondered what life would be like without these machines? Not so long ago, people used clunky telephones that they could not take outside. They used loud typewriters to type reports. They wrote letters to friends using pen and paper!

Computers have been around since the 1950s. Back then, computers worked very slowly and were as big as a room! Today's computers are more powerful. They are faster and smaller, too. Now we can surf the Internet, print photographs, and write to our friends—all on a computer. It's all just a click away!

The first computers filled a whole room.

Words with *ou* and *ow*

Activity One

About Words with *ou* and *ow*

When you see the letters *ou* or *ow* together in words, they often have the vowel sound you hear in *mouse* and *cow*. As your teacher reads *What Was Once New*, listen carefully for words containing this vowel sound. Here are other words to know: *ground, couch, scout, proud, owl, brown, plow, crown.*

Words with *ou* and *ow* in Context

With a partner, reread *What Was Once New* and look for words with *ou* or *ow*. Sort the words and write them in two lists. When you are finished, compare your list with another partner team's.

Activity Two

Explore Words Together

Work with a small group to come up with funny sentences using words with *ou* or *ow*. Use the words listed on the right to help you get started. Share your group's sentences with the whole class.

howl	cloud
clown	hound
crowd	mouth

Activity Three

Explore Words in Writing

Write a short paragraph about technology that you use every day. Use as many words with *ou* and *ow* as possible from the activities above. Have a partner circle all the words with *ou* or *ow* that make the sound you hear in *cow*.

Female FIRSTS

Meet Amelia Bloomer, Susan B. Anthony, Shirley Chisholm, and Dianne Feinstein

by Michelle Sale

Amelia Bloomer

Only 100 years ago, most women were not allowed to vote. They often could not get an education. Four amazing females helped make life better for women.

AMELIA BLOOMER (1818–1894)

Amelia Bloomer thought that women should make their own decisions. In the 1800s, women wore long, heavy skirts. Bloomer wanted comfortable clothing. She wore baggy pants with shorter skirts. Many women liked this new look. They called the pants "bloomers."

In 1849, Bloomer started a newspaper called *The Lily. The Lily* supported women's right to vote. After reading the paper, many women joined the fight for the right to vote.

> What strategies could you use to help you understand this page?

SUSAN B. ANTHONY (1820–1906)

Susan B. Anthony was a friend of Amelia Bloomer's. Like Bloomer, Anthony believed strongly in women's rights.

In 1868, Anthony started her own newspaper. She wanted to share her views with others. Anthony was angry. Women were not treated the same as men. No one listened to them on important issues.

To make big changes, women had to be able to vote. The law didn't say women could not vote. But it didn't say that they could, either.

Anthony voted in the 1872 Presidential election. She was arrested. This didn't stop her time line for reform. From 1869 through 1906, Anthony spoke to every new Congress. She asked them to pass a law that let women vote.

In 1920 her hard work paid off. The law was changed. American women have voted ever since.

Susan B. Anthony

Do you see any words or ideas you don't understand? How can you figure out the meanings?

In 1979, Anthony's face appeared on the new dollar coin. She was the first woman to appear on American money.

SHIRLEY CHISHOLM (1924–2005)

Shirley Chisholm was the first African American woman elected to Congress. She was also the first woman to run for President. Without the work of women like Bloomer and Anthony, Chisholm could never have done these things!

Partner Jigsaw Technique Read a section of the biographies with a partner and write down one strategy you used to monitor your understanding. Be prepared to summarize your section and share one strategy.

At first Chisholm worked locally. She won a seat in the New York State Assembly. She worked to get funds for day-care centers and schools.

In 1968, Chisholm was elected to Congress. Her election showed a shift in voters' attitudes toward women. Chisholm was re-elected and served a total of 14 years.

In 1972, Chisholm ran for President. She didn't win. But she was a role model. Chisholm said, "I ran because somebody had to do it first. In this country everybody is supposed to be able to run for President."

Chisholm gave women hope that someday a woman could be President.

What reading strategies did you use to help you understand the importance of Chisholm's work?

Shirley Chisholm

DIANNE FEINSTEIN
(1933–present)

The work of Bloomer, Anthony, and Chisholm helped Dianne Feinstein. Feinstein became the first female mayor of San Francisco in 1978.

Feinstein was mayor for 10 years. She created jobs. She cleaned up the city and made it safer.

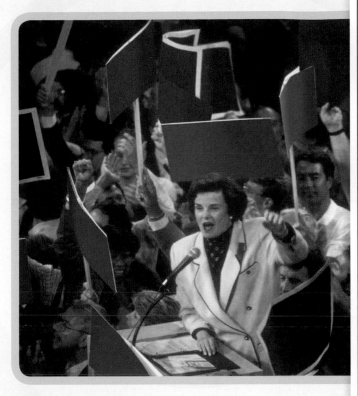

Dianne Feinstein

In 1990 Feinstein lost a close race for Governor of California. In 1992, she was elected to the U.S. Senate as the first female Senator from California.

Now she works to fight crime and care for natural resources. In a speech that Feinstein gave on International Women's Day in 2005, she asked the President to think about women's issues around the world. She said, "I truly believe it is our duty . . . to address and seek workable solutions to every problem that women face around the world. We can—and we must."

> What strategies could you use to help you understand Feinstein's speech? Explain.

Women's Firsts in U. S. History

This list of dates shows some important events and people in the history of women's rights.

1848—Women hold the first Women's Rights Convention in Seneca Falls, New York. This is the start of the movement for women's rights in the United States.

1920—After years of protest and hard work, women win the right to vote. The 19th Amendment to the Constitution becomes law.

1935—Mary McLeod Bethune starts the National Council of Negro Women. This group fights unfair treatment of African Americans and women.

Mary McLeod Bethune

1961—Former First Lady Eleanor Roosevelt heads the President's Commission on the Status of Women. The President's Commission recommends that women be paid the same as men for doing equal work.

What strategy would be most helpful to you in understanding the information on this page?

1981—Sandra Day O'Connor is the first woman appointed to the Supreme Court.

1984—Geraldine Ferraro is the first woman to run for vice president on a major-party ticket.

Geraldine Ferraro

Think and Respond

Reflect and Write

- You and your partner have read sections of *Female Firsts*. Discuss the strategies you used to help you understand the text.

- On one side of an index card, describe a part of your reading you found difficult to understand. On the other side, write the strategies you used to make the meaning clear. Find another partner team that read different sections and share your strategies.

Words with *ou, ow* in Context

Search through *Female Firsts* to find all the words with *ou* and *ow* that have the vowel sound heard in *cow*. Write down the words you find and then circle the vowel sound in each word.

Sandra Day O'Connor

Turn and Talk

MONITOR UNDERSTANDING

Discuss with a partner what you have learned so far about monitoring understanding.

- How do you monitor understanding as you read?

Look at page 141. Discuss with your partner what may be difficult to understand. Talk about the strategies that can help you.

Critical Thinking

In a group, discuss the concerns of Bloomer and Anthony long ago and the concerns of Chisholm and Feinstein. Write one concern for each pair of women. Then answer these questions.

- How have women's concerns changed from long ago? Why?

- Have things changed for women between the times of Bloomer and Feinstein? Why or why not?

ROLLER COASTERS:
Past to Present

The **time line** for roller coasters began long ago. In the 1600s, huge ice slides were built in Russia. By the 1800s, roller coasters had cars and tracks. They were made of wood. They had sharp turns and steep drops.

By the 1920s, wooden roller coaster could go up to 60 miles per hour.

The 1950s brought a **shift** in how coasters were built. Some new roller coasters were made of steel. Steel can be bent and shaped at a **factory**. Builders could make coasters taller, smoother, and faster. Riders could **appreciate** the new thrills. So roller coasters continued to get bigger and better. Today some are more than 450 feet tall. Riders go nearly 130 miles per hour! Steel helped **expand** the world of roller coasters.

A bigger and better roller coaster

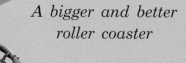

Structured Vocabulary Discussion

After your teacher reads these sentences, say the vocabulary word that comes to mind. Discuss your choices with a partner.

My grandfather puts together cars in a _____.

Putting events in order creates a _____.

Changing your mind shows a _____ in your thinking.

Throughout the week, add to your vocabulary journal entries. Record new insights and other words that relate to this week's vocabulary.

Picture It

Copy this chart into your vocabulary journal. Give examples of things that **expand**. Then write words that mean about the same as **expand**.

things that expand	words that mean the same as expand
balloon	get bigger

Copy this word web into your vocabulary journal. Give examples of things that family members or friends do for you that you **appreciate**.

appreciate

make lunch

Genre
Photo Essay

The Telephone: It's Come a Long Way

by Clyde Wolf

New machines bring big changes. But change doesn't stop there. People keep making machines better. The telephone is a good example.

1877

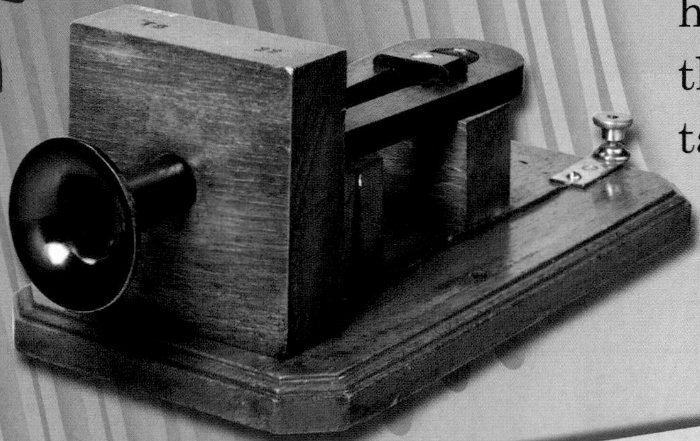

The first telephone had a round opening that was used for both talking and listening.

1913

A caller told a telephone operator the number to use or the person to call. Then the operator made the call and connected the two people.

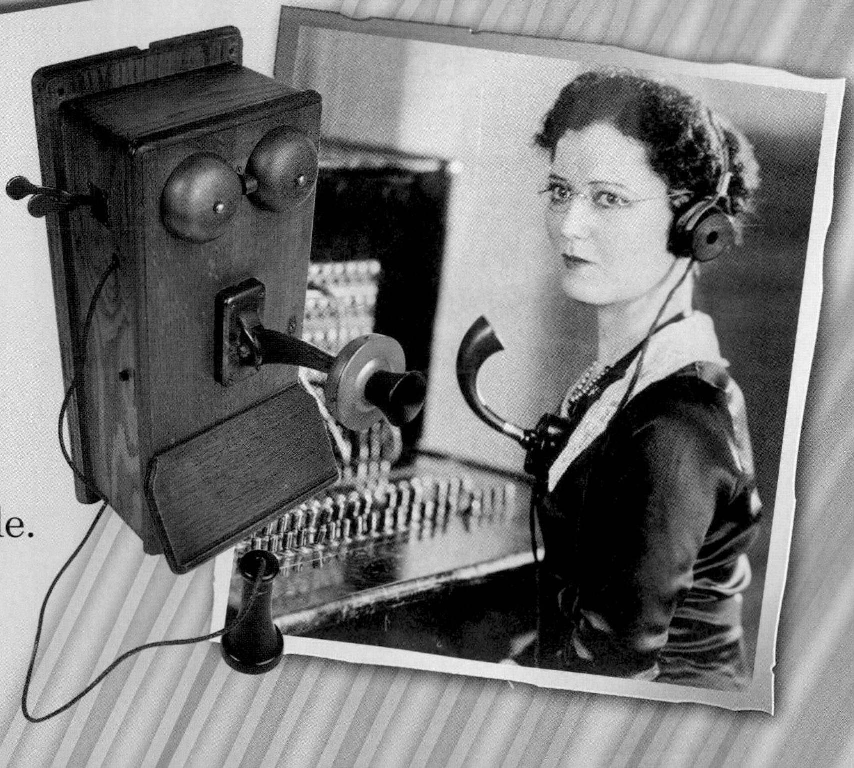

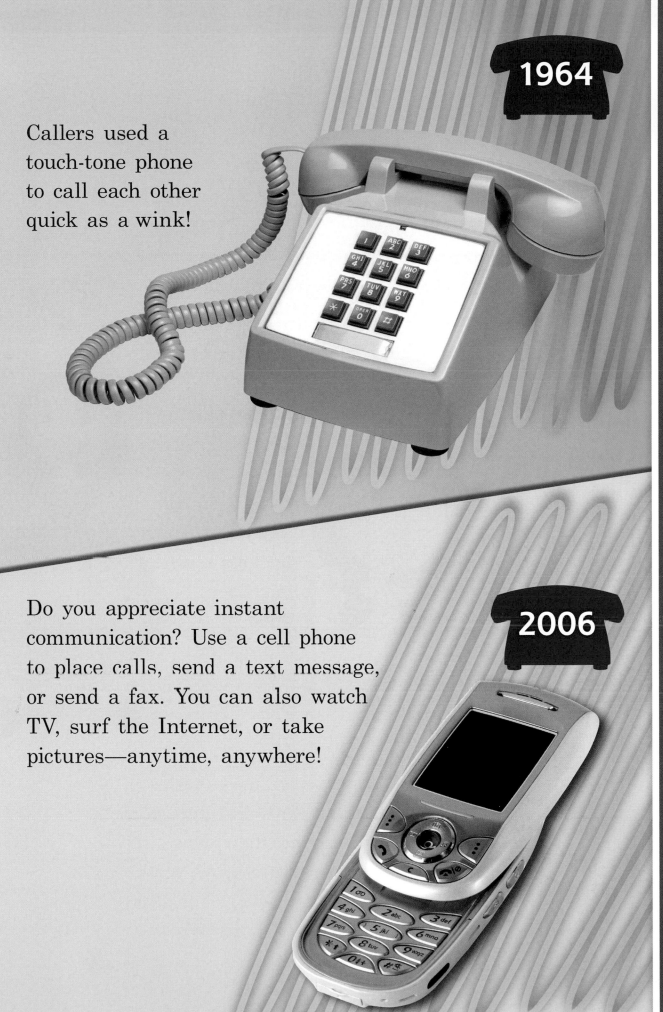

1964

Callers used a touch-tone phone to call each other quick as a wink!

2006

Do you appreciate instant communication? Use a cell phone to place calls, send a text message, or send a fax. You can also watch TV, surf the Internet, or take pictures—anytime, anywhere!

What Were They Thinking?

"Fashion Flashbacks" is a new TV series on fashion history. It will make you glad you didn't live long ago! The first episode looks at what children wore more than a hundred years ago. Enjoy this show tonight at seven. Here are some highlights.

Pudding caps:

You didn't eat them! Toddlers wore these padded hats to protect their heads. Talk about spoiling your hairdo!

Hoop skirts:

The hoop skirts girls wore may have been fun. They had secret pockets sewn into them, great for hiding toys.

Stays: Stays were curved strips of bone or wood. Boys and girls both wore them around their waists to develop good posture. Boys wore long pants by age seven, but girls toiled with stays all their lives.

Words with *oy* and *oi*

Activity One

About Words with *oy* and *oi*

When you see *oy* or *oi* together in words, they make the vowel sound you hear in *boy*. As your teacher reads *What Were They Thinking?* listen for words with the *oy* sound. Here are other words to know that have the same *oy* vowel sound: *enjoy, royal, annoy, oyster, point, soil, oil, boil.*

Words with *oy* and *oi* in Context

Work with a partner to find the *oy* and *oi* words in *What Were They Thinking?* Make a list of the words. Compare your list with another partner team's.

Pudding Cap

Activity Two

Explore Words Together

coin	noise
toy	poison
choice	destroy

With a partner, read the words in the box at the right. Together write two sentences that each use an *oi* and *oy* word from the box. Read your sentences out loud to the other teams.

Activity Three

Explore Words in Writing

Use the words from the first two activities and any other *oy* or *oi* words to write about a television show you like. Exchange your writing with a partner and read each other's sentences. Count the number of *oy* and *oi* words you both used.

An Adventure in Time

By Cynthia Mercati

We boarded the bus at school for the Springdale Historical Museum. Our class was going to spend the whole day learning about the history of our town.

The first exhibit at the museum was about the frontier. My friend Miguel and I stopped short in front of a life-sized model of a covered wagon. *What would it feel like to sit on that?* I wondered.

Miguel and I were the only ones from the class left in the room. We both pulled ourselves up on the wagon bench, and I lifted the reins.

"Giddyup!" I called to my imaginary oxen. That's when we suddenly heard a voice from the dark canvas opening behind us.

"Quit lollygaggin', you two," a woman said. "Pa and I are waitin' to go!"

What do you think has happened to the students at the museum? What clue does the title of the story give you?

"Yes, ma'am," Miguel and I muttered, surprised.

We jumped out of the wagon. The museum had disappeared, and the great prairie stretched out in front of us! Real oxen were hitched to the wagon. I was wearing a bonnet and a long calico dress with an apron over it! Miguel was wearing brown pants and a homemade calico shirt. Both of us were barefoot!

What details on this page give you a new idea about what is happening to the two children?

"We must have passed through some kind of time machine," I whispered, excited.

"We have ten miles to do today!" Pa shouted.

"Woo-hoo," Ma said, "We're on our way to Springdale! You kids start walking."

"Springdale?" Miguel and I echoed.

"It's a mighty fine place for a homestead," said Pa.

"Springdale," I mumbled as we started walking, "how annoying."

Later we stopped for lunch, or the "nooning," as Pa called it. Miguel and I were sent to fetch water and gather wood. We had no choice.

Say Something Technique Take turns reading a section of text, covering it up, and then saying something about it to your partner. You may say any thought or idea that the text brings to your mind.

After lunch, we started up again. I picked wildflowers and knotted their stems together. I added more and more flowers to expand my wreath. Smiling, I slipped it around my neck and enjoyed the sweet smell. This sure was better than anything that was made in a factory.

I gazed around at the rolling hills. The past *was* pretty. However, we hadn't even had an adventure yet. That was about to change. A river stood right in our path.

Pa cut two long poles from the cottonwood trees growing by the water's edge. He handed one to me and one to Ma.

"You two will have to pole the wagon across like a raft," he said. "Then the boy and I will swim the oxen across."

What new idea do you have about the family in this story from the details on this page?

154

Ma stuck her pole into the water. I gritted my teeth and did the same. Butterflies were in my stomach.

We reached the middle of the river. The boiling rapids suddenly gripped the wagon and turned it around. We tipped from side to side, water splashing up over the sides.

This is it, Lucinda, I told myself. *You're having your adventure! I just hope you survive it!* I didn't feel excited—just scared.

We worked hard with our poles, and before you knew it, we were on the other side!

"Good work, daughter," Ma said.

Pa and Miguel plunged the oxen into the river. Miguel held on to an ox and used his other hand to swim. They looked like toys in the river.

When Miguel got safely to the other side, I gave him a high-five. "We did it!"

Maybe that was the point of having adventures, I thought, *learning something about yourself. Learning that you could do something difficult!*

What do the details on this page tell you about the adventures of Miguel and Lucinda?

"Fetch us some blankets, children," Ma said.

I swung myself into the back of the wagon. Miguel joined me.

It was pitch dark again. As we pushed aside the canvas opening to come back out, we found ourselves back in the museum. We were back in our own time again!

Miguel shook his head as if trying to clear it of any confusion. "Wow," he breathed.

"Wow is right," I agreed, "weird—but cool!"

Mrs. Fisher was waiting for us in the next room. We'd been in the past almost the whole day, but not much time had passed in the present. How could that be? *I must have dreamed the whole thing!* I thought.

As I walked into the next room, Mrs. Fisher stopped me.

"Where did you get this wreath?" she asked, puzzled.

My hand flew to my neck to touch the necklace. My mouth dropped open and my stomach lurched. *Now, where had I gotten it?*

Based on the details, what do you think Lucinda and Miguel learned from their adventure?

Think and Respond

Reflect and Write

- You and your partner have read parts of *An Adventure in Time*. Discuss what each of you thought about after reading each section.

- On one side of an index card, write details from a section of the story. On the other side, write how the details help you understand something new about Lucinda and Miguel's adventure.

Words with *oy* and *oi* in Context

Search through *An Adventure in Time* for all the words with *oy* and *oi*. Write down the words you find, and share your list with a partner.

Turn and Talk

SYNTHESIZE

Discuss with a partner what you have learned so far about synthesizing information.

- How does synthesizing help you understand a selection?

- Choose two important details on page 156. With a partner, discuss how these details help you form a new idea.

Critical Thinking

With a partner, brainstorm what you might see if you visited the early days of your hometown. Write your ideas on the right side of a sheet of paper. On the left side write what Lucinda and Miguel see. Then answer these questions.

- How are things in the past different from things today? How are they the same?

- What can people do now that they couldn't do in the past?

Contents

Modeled Reading

Shared Reading

Interactive Reading

True Heart

Marissa Moss
Illustrated by C. F. Payne

Strategic Listening

Strategic listening means listening for words that create images in your mind. Listen to the focus questions your teacher will read to you.

Time Flies —
On Japan's Trains!

A Shinkansen train

Shinkansen trains are Japan's high-speed "bullet" trains. They are famous for their high speed and **elegant** design. This railway **technology** lets people travel in record time. **Construction** of the Shinkansen was completed in 1964. The trains went 125 miles per hour. Today they go almost 200 miles per hour! The Shinkansen is a part of Japan's **transit** system. It's a great way to explore Japan's mountain **frontier**.

You can take the Shinkansen to Nagano. This line opened when Nagano hosted the Olympics in 1998. Nagano is now just an hour and a half from Japan's capital. The same trip used to take more than three hours!

Structured Vocabulary Discussion

In a small group, complete the following sentences about your vocabulary words. Compare your sentences with those of another group.

Some forms of *transit* are . . .

Technology and *frontier* are different because . . .

Three examples of things that are *elegant* are . . .

Throughout the week, add to your vocabulary journal entries. Record new insights and other words that relate to this week's vocabulary.

Picture It

Copy this word web into your vocabulary journal. Fill in the circles with things you might see on a **frontier.**

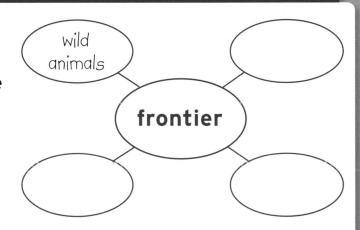

Copy this word wheel into your vocabulary journal. Write the first words that you think of when you see the word **technology.**

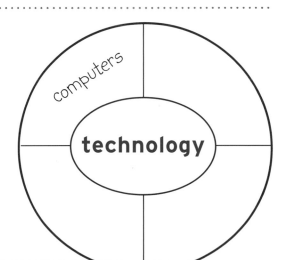

Comprehension Strategy

Create Images

Create mental **IMAGES** as you read.

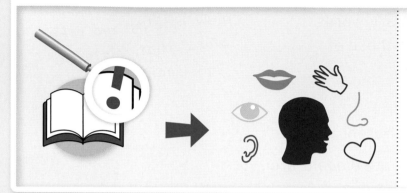

Think about how something might look, feel, smell, sound, or taste to help you make a picture in your mind.

TURN AND TALK Listen as your teacher reads about Bee's first ride as engineer in *True Heart* and models how to create images. Then discuss answers to these questions.

- What does Bee see, hear, smell, touch, and taste?
- Which words help you create pictures in your mind.

TAKE IT WITH YOU As you read other selections, try to create as many mental images as you can. Use a chart like the one below to record details that help you create images in your mind as you read.

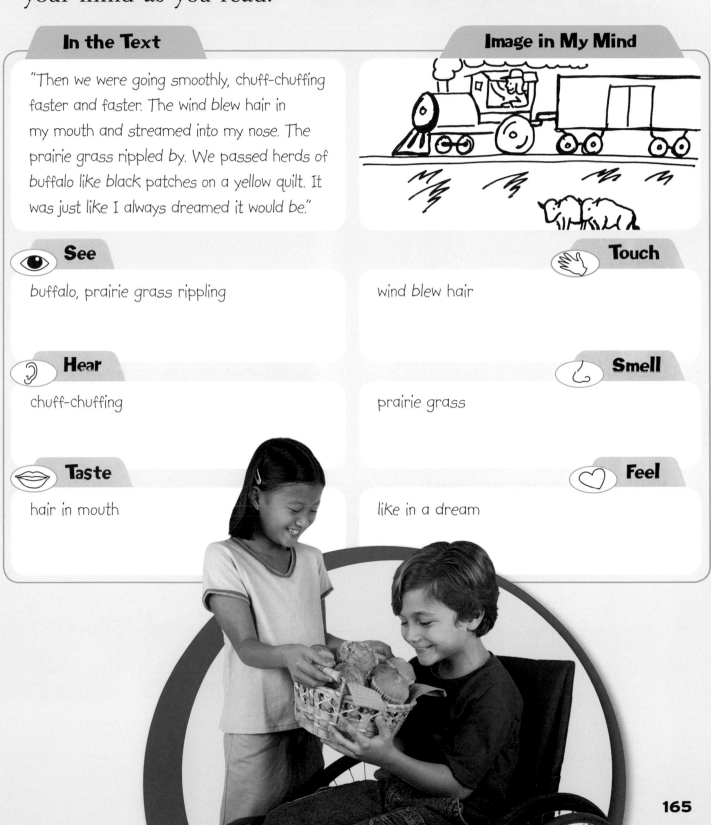

In the Text

"Then we were going smoothly, chuff-chuffing faster and faster. The wind blew hair in my mouth and streamed into my nose. The prairie grass rippled by. We passed herds of buffalo like black patches on a yellow quilt. It was just like I always dreamed it would be."

Image in My Mind

See

buffalo, prairie grass rippling

Touch

wind blew hair

Hear

chuff-chuffing

Smell

prairie grass

Taste

hair in mouth

Feel

like in a dream

Helicopter Rescue at Sea

by Amanda Cunningham

Kauai, Hawaii—Nov. 3

Thursday night off Kauai's North Shore, Bruce Camara of Kilauea was in trouble. A U.S. Coast Guard helicopter rescued Camara after a flash flood carried him out to sea.

Camara was working on his small boat on Kilauea Stream. The severe rainstorm hit around 6 P.M. Soon after this, Camara found himself in the water. He was swept into the ocean by the flood rush.

"The water came through town like a wave and just washed through everything," said witness Christine Marten. When she saw what happened to Camara, she called 911.

A Kauai police rescue team tried to get to Camara from the shore. But the wind and rain made it too hard to reach him. The water was also moving too fast for rescue boats.

U.S. Coast Guard helicopter rescues person at sea.

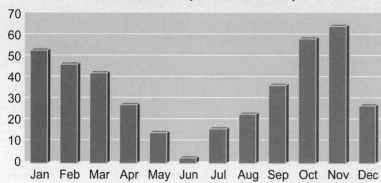

TOTAL NUMBER OF FLASH FLOODS IN HAWAII (1960–2005)

| Jan | Feb | Mar | Apr | May | Jun | Jul | Aug | Sep | Oct | Nov | Dec |

The number of flash floods by month in Hawaii, 1960–2005. Most flash floods occur from September to March.

At about 6:30 P.M., a Coast Guard helicopter arrived. Rescue swimmer David Morse was lowered in a metal basket on a long cable. Morse dove into the water. He pulled Camara to the basket, and helped him get in. Then the basket was lifted to the helicopter.

"Camara was starting to get numb," said Morse. "He did well to hang on in the water for almost half an hour. The currents were very strong."

County officials want to buy other forms of transportation for flood rescues. Some cars and boats can go from driving on a road to floating on a flooded river. Rafts that are operated like a kite by someone on land can save a person stuck in deep or fast water. The floating helicopter basket that Camara was rescued in holds up to 16 people.

"Rescuers need to have the right equipment," Officer Morse pointed out. "Thanks to improvements in rescue transportation, Mr. Camara has a whole new adventure to share."

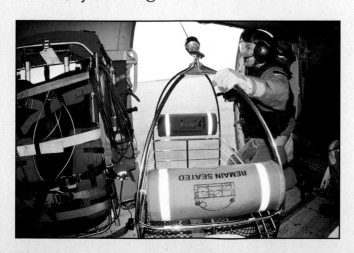

Rescue basket

Word Study

✉ SEND   💾 SAVE   🗑 TRASH   📎 ATTACHMENT

To: Keesha Jackson
Cc:

Subject: Great Dude Ranch Vacation!!

▶ Attachments: *Horseback Riding.jpg*

ab/ab | Font ▼ | Font Size ▼ | **B** *I* U T | ☰ ☰ ☰

Date: Tue, 21 Mar 2007 05:41 P.M.

Keesha, I'm writing you from Flagstaff, Arizona. The dude ranch where we're staying is amazing. By the time I get home, I will have ridden in or on everything there is!

I'm having a whole lot of fun! We hiked into a canyon down a steep, narrow trail. I also did some rock climbing. Yesterday I rode a horse for the first time. It's not as easy as it looks, even though the horse was as gentle as a lamb.

We also rode in a very bumpy horse-drawn wagon to a ghost town. I'm glad to live in the 21st century with smooth roads. ☺

Tomorrow, we're going river rafting. Who knows what adventures we'll have! I'll tell you all about it when I get home—after 8 long and slow hours on a train! ☹

Your friend,
Bernard

Silent Consonants
w, *h*, and *b*

Activity One

About Silent Consonants *w*, *h*, and *b*

The letter *w* is sometimes silent in some words, as in *writer*. An *h* is silent in some words, such as *ghost*. The letter *b* is not pronounced after the letter *m* when they are in the same syllable, such as *thumb*. As your teacher reads the email, read along and look for letters that are not pronounced. Here are other examples of words that have the silent *w*, *h*, and *b*: *who, wrote, wrench, wrap, hour, comb.*

Silent Consonants *w*, *h*, and *b* in Context

Reread the passage, looking for words with a silent *w*, *h*, and *b*. Write the words with these silent letters in a list. Then compare your lists with a partner's.

Activity Two

Explore Words Together

With a partner, copy the words on the right and underline the silent letter in each word. Sort each word into the correct silent *w*, *h*, or *b* word group, as above.

honest	rhyme
climb	whose
whoever	plumber

Activity Three

Explore Words in Writing

Write your own short letter about your favorite way to travel. Use words from Activities One and Two. Exchange letters with a partner and circle all the words you find with silent *w*, *h*, and *b*.

A Family Journey

by Annie Choi

Jay tightened his seatbelt and gripped the armrests until his hands were almost numb. His heart pounded so loud that he thought everyone on the plane could hear it. He had never been on a plane before.

"Don't worry," said his mother. "Everyone gets a little nervous at takeoff."

The engines started to roar, and the plane started moving faster and faster. Then finally, it lifted off!

Jay looked out the window. Thousands of buildings dotted the ground beneath him. He tried to look for his house, but didn't know where to begin. White clouds drifted around the plane's wings.

"How long until we get to Korea?" Jay asked.

"Fourteen hours," said Jay's father.

"Wow," Jay said. "That's like two whole days of school!"

> What words on this page help you to have a picture in your mind about Jay on the plane?

"Wake up, Jay, we're here!" Jay's mother said as she combed her hair.

Inside the terminal, a security officer looked at their passports and smiled.

"Welcome to Seoul, South Korea." He stamped their passports. "Enjoy your stay!"

Jay's mother led the way to the airport meeting area.

"There he is!" she yelled. Jay turned his head and saw his uncle Lee waving his arms wildly. Jay's mother ran ahead and hugged her brother.

Uncle Lee asked Jay, "Are you ready for the *ji-ha-chol*? That's the subway in Korean. It's a lot like the one in New York City, but more crowded!"

What pictures do you have in your mind of Jay at the airport?

"It's rush hour. Are you up for an adventure?" Jay's father grinned at his son.

They entered the subway tunnel and hundreds of people rushed around them. Jay had never seen so many people in one place in his entire life.

"It's like a whole city, only underground!" Jay pointed to stores and restaurants in the tunnel.

"You can get everything here," Lee replied, "from bicycles to dried squid."

The subway doors opened, and a river of people came flowing out of the train car. Then Jay and his family scrambled in.

"We're packed in like sardines!" Jay said.

The train snaked its way through dark tunnels underneath Seoul. After a while, Jay's uncle announced, "We're getting off at the next stop!"

Say Something Technique
Take turns reading a section of text, covering it up, and then saying something about it to your partner. You may say any thought or idea that the text brings to your mind.

What details help you create a mental image of the *ji-ah-chul*?

They climbed the stairs out of the subway station. The sound of whirring engines, honking horns, and sirens filled the air. Motorized scooters seemed to buzz everywhere like bees in a hive.

Cars, taxis, and buses filled the wide streets that wrapped around the city. Almost as many people rode bicycles. Now that was a sight!

Jay saw a tiny truck whiz by. It looked like a toy.

"That's called a *bongo*!" said Uncle Lee. "On these crowded streets, smaller is better."

What mental images do you have of the different kinds of transportation Jay sees on the streets of Seoul?

"Some people still use rickshaws to get around," said Jay's mother. "They are like carts with passengers pulled by a person on foot," she told Jay.

"We have to hop on the next bus," said Uncle Lee. Luckily, the bus wasn't as crowded as the subway, and Jay took a seat near the front.

Department stores, markets, and restaurants lined the busy streets. Men and women stood outside of stores and passed out brightly colored fliers. One was dressed in a tiger costume.

Slowly the busy streets melted away. The bus drove through a quiet neighborhood surrounded by fields of agriculture. A small vegetable stand and a restaurant stood on the corner. A few kids were playing soccer in the street.

"This is our stop," said Jay's uncle.

"We've been traveling for a long time," said Jay's mother, smiling. "I've lost count of the hours."

They walked up a small, quiet street.

"Here we are at home," said Jay's uncle.

Jay smiled at his family. "We're home," he repeated. He couldn't wait to go to bed and wake up to another exciting day.

What picture do you have in your mind of Jay at the end of the story?

174

Think and Respond

Reflect and Write

- You and your partner have read *A Family Journey*. Discuss with your partner the thoughts and ideas you had.

- On one side of an index card, write several images you formed as your read. On the other side, write the details from the story that helped you form the pictures in your mind.

Silent Consonants *w*, *h*, and *b* in Context

Search through *A Family Journey* to find words with a silent *w*, *h* or *b* and make a list. Write a new sentence with each word.

Turn and Talk

CREATE IMAGES

Discuss with a partner what you have learned so far about creating images.

- How can creating images help you understand the text?

Picture in your mind the streets of Seoul, Korea. Write words that describe your mental image of the city. Discuss your words with your partner.

Critical Thinking

With a partner, make a list of different kinds of transportation. Return to *A Family Journey* and list the forms of transportation in the text. Then answer these questions.

- How was the transportation used in the story similar to or different from the transportation you use?

- Why do you think people use so many kinds of transportation?

TRAVEL IN THE Year 3200

Marsha's new pod was the latest design.

Marsha flew to school in her brand new pod. It was a present from her parents. The pod was special because it ran on plant fuel. **Agriculture** was important to her family. They had a farm. They grew plants for food, and made **fuel** from what was left over. Marsha, however, was more interested in **aviation**. She loved to fly!

"I'm ready for an **adventure**. I'm going to **explore**," Marsha said to her friends as she flew off from school. Minutes later, her pod was out of fuel. She had forgotten to fill up the tank. Then Marsha remembered that she had lunch with her. Veggies for two!

Filling up.

Structured Vocabulary Discussion

Work with a partner or in a small group to fill in each blank with a vocabulary word. When you're finished, share your answers with the class. Be sure you can explain how the words are related.

Food is to *person* as _____ is to *automobile*.

A *walk* is to a *hike* as a *trip* is to an _____.

Look is to *find* as _____ is to *discover*.

Throughout the week, add to your vocabulary journal entries. Record new insights and other words that relate to this week's vocabulary.

Picture It

Copy this word web into your vocabulary journal. Give examples of things or places people **explore**.

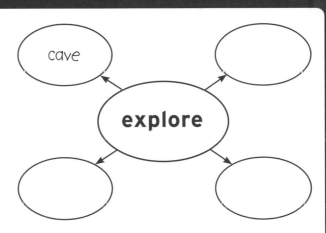

Copy this word wheel into your vocabulary journal. Write ideas or words you think of when you see the word **adventure**.

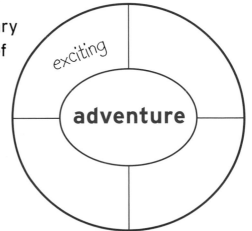

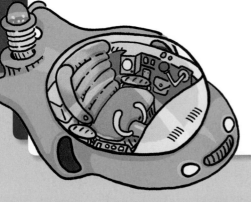

The First Flight

by Maryann MacDonald

It was September, 1783,
when we made history,
the rooster, the hen, and me.

We were set in a basket
and tied to a silk balloon.
Feeding a fire with wool,
straw and old shoes,
two brothers filled
the balloon with hot air
until it rose up,

up,
Up,
Up!

high above the French king,
higher still above his palace.

Floating along in the breeze,

we traveled eight miles.

Cluck-cluck! said the worried hen.

Cock-a-doodle-doo! screeched the rooster.

As for me, I could only bleat, *Baaa!*

We were the first to fly,

in a man-made machine—

the first to explore the clouds,

to see the ribbon rivers below,

and houses that looked like grains of corn.

WILD WAYS TO GO!

Transportation comes in many forms. Here are some ways to get around that you just don't see every day. Without a doubt, you can have the ride of your life!

Would you like a ride in a *tuk-tuk*? These three-wheelers have room for a driver and three people in the back. They are named after the sound the engine makes.

How about a racecar? These cars top 220 miles per hour! Tight turns force drivers to make all the right moves to keep the car safely on the track. There are no road signs.

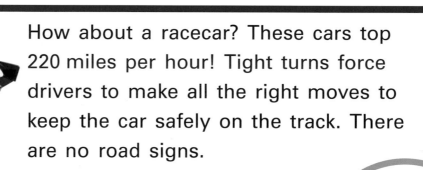

How would you like to take a flight on an airplane going 2,200 miles per hour? A plane called a Blackbird can travel this fast and fly above 80,000 feet.

Silent Consonants
b, *g*, and *gh*

Activity One

About Silent Consonants
b, *g*, and *gh*

The letter *b* is silent when it appears in a word before *t*, such as in *debt*. The letter *g* is silent before *n*, such as in *design*. The letters *gh* are silent in words such as *sigh* and *night*. As your teacher reads the selection, read along and look for letters *b*, *g*, and *gh* that are not pronounced. Here are other words to know with the silent consonants *b*, *g*, and *gh: doubt, debt, subtle, sign, gnat, design, sleigh, dough, eight, sight.*

Silent Consonants *b*, *g*, and *gh* In Context

Reread the passage with a partner. Make a list of all the words you find that have the silent consonants *b*, *g*, and *gh*. Write the words in three lists. Discuss your findings.

Activity Two

Explore Words Together

sigh	gnaw
debt	fight
through	foreign

With a partner, sort the words on the right into the correct silent consonant groups, as above. List any other words you know with the same silent consonants.

Activity Three

Explore Words in Writing

With your partner, write a paragraph about your favorite way to travel. Include several words with silent consonants *b*, *g*, and *gh*. Then exchange with another partner team and circle the words with those silent consonants.

ZOOMING into the FUTURE!

An Interview with Paul Hernandez

by Molly Smith

How do you think people will get around in the future? Can you picture yourself buzzing high in the sky with a rocket pack? Would you like to cruise *above* the road in a hover car? These forms of transportation may sound like science fiction. But they may be more real than you think! Just ask Paul Hernandez.

Paul Hernandez is a manager of the Transportation Library at the University of California, Berkeley. He helps people find information on transportation. The library has more than two hundred thousand books. Paul makes sure people can find the book they need.

We talked to Hernandez about forms of transportation of yesterday, today, and tomorrow.

What strategies could you use to help you understand this page?

What transportation invention changed lives the most?

I think trains changed lives the most. Before trains, people never moved faster than a horse could gallop. Suddenly, anyone with a train ticket could travel great distances at higher speeds.

What kind of transportation has changed the most since it was invented?

I think cars have changed the most. Cars today have some of the same basic parts as the first cars. They still have four wheels. They still have a steering wheel and brakes. However, in new cars, computers now control all the parts. There is no doubt cars are also much safer than they were a hundred years ago.

What strategies could you use to monitor your understanding of the changes in transportation?

Why don't some ideas for new kinds of transportation work?

Good ideas often fail because they cost too much. A single airplane needs special fuel, an aviation pilot, spare parts, and runways. These things cost a lot of money. A new transportation design needs many people who will help pay to build it.

Reverse Think-Aloud Technique
Listen as your partner reads part of the text aloud. Choose a point in the text to stop your partner and ask what he or she is thinking about the text at that moment. Then switch roles with your partner.

What do you predict people will be riding around in one hundred years from now?

I think that personal rapid transit will exist. Personal rapid transit (PRT) will be like the subway. But you will not wait at the station for the train. You won't have to read any signs. Instead there will be personal cars. When you get in, you just tell a computer where you want to go. The car will go straight there. The idea has been around for more than fifty years, but it still costs too much money.

What strategies could you use to help you understand more about PRT? Explain.

Do you think someone will invent rocket packs or a flying car?

Rocket packs have already been built! However, they are difficult to fly. Rocket packs can stay in the air for only a few seconds. Flying cars have been built, too. They are called "hover cars." They use too much fuel, and are also hard to steer.

I really like magnetic levitation, or "maglev." These amazing trains float above the track. They use magnets and electricity for power. They are safer than other trains. Some countries, such as China, Japan, and Germany, have already started building and using maglev trains.

How is a maglev train different than other trains?

What makes them safer?

Maglev trains have no contact with the tracks. So they won't run off the tracks. The trains are supported by magnetic fields. The ride is quieter and smoother than in an airplane.

Will regular people ever be able to travel to space?

Yes, but right now it costs a lot of money to get there.

What word or idea on this page were you not sure about the first time you read it? What strategy did you use to figure out the meaning?

Is there a way to make space travel less expensive in the future?

Maybe one day we will build a space elevator. The space elevator would be like a very strong ribbon. It would be attached to the Earth at one end and to a satellite at the other. It would be more than 22,000 miles long. The space elevator would have robotic cars climbing up and down it!

What is your dream form of transportation?

My dream transportation would be people transporters. They would zap people from one place to another. Travel would take no time at all. Great distances would not be the problem they are today.

Because travel would be easier, people would travel more. The world would not seem like such a big place. People of different countries would start seeing each other as part of the same community. Now that would be a dream come true!

Think and Respond

Reflect and Write

- You and your partner have read and discussed sections of *Zooming Into the Future!* Talk with your partner about what each of you thought as you read.

- Choose one page from the interview. On one side of an index card, write a list of things you do not understand. On the other side, write the strategies that would better help you understand the interview.

Silent Consonants *b*, *g*, and *gh* in Context

Find words in the interview with silent consonants *b*, *g*, and *gh*. Then write your own sentences using each word.

Turn and Talk

MONITOR UNDERSTANDING

Discuss with a partner what you have learned about how to monitor understanding.

- Why is it important to monitor understanding?

Look at the last page of the interview. Discuss the strategies you used to help you understand the page.

Critical Thinking

With a partner, discuss one kind of transportation from the interview that you think people will use in the future. Write your ideas to tell why it will be used. Then answer these questions.

- How do you think transportation has changed since your grandparents were your age?

- How do you think transportation will change in the future?

The Great Wave Off Kanagawa, 1826–33
Katsushika Hokusai (1760–1849)

UNIT: Forces of *Nature*

THEME **7** **On Moving Ground**

THEME **8** **Predicting Nature's Hazards**

Viewing

This painting is one of a series. Kanagawa is an area in the foothills of Mt. Fuji. The Japanese artist made 35 other paintings of Mount Fuji, which is shown in the background. Hokusai was a woodblock artist. The paintings were made by carving blocks of wood, painting them, and pressing the wood onto paper.

1. What do you see in the picture? How does the picture show motion?

2. What do you think caused this wave? What effects do you think it might have when it reaches the shore of Kanagawa?

3. How do you think the people in the boats feel about the wave?

In This UNIT

In this unit, you will read about forces of nature, such as earthquakes and volcanoes. You will also read about predicting dangerous weather, such as tornadoes and hurricanes.

Contents

On Moving Ground

Into the Volcano

by Donna O'Meara

Critical Listening

Critical listening means listening for facts and opinions. Listen to the focus questions your teacher will read to you.

Look Out for Lava!

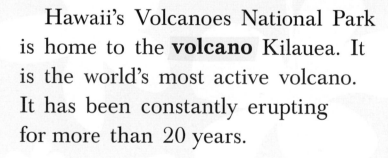

Tourists come to see nature's show.

Lava spills into the sea.

Hawaii's Volcanoes National Park is home to the **volcano** Kilauea. It is the world's most active volcano. It has been constantly erupting for more than 20 years.

The park is a **favorite** place for tourists. Scientists also visit. They come to study volcanoes. They want to learn how to **anticipate** when a volcano will erupt. Visitors soon **realize** that the **surface** of our planet is always changing!

Kilauea puts on a spectacular show.

anticipate   realize   favorite   surface   volcano

Structured Vocabulary Discussion

Read the words and phrases shown below. Pick one vocabulary word to go with each word or phrase. Explain why you chose each word.

top

I can hardly wait

the color you like best

eruption

now I understand

Throughout the week, add to your vocabulary journal entries. Record new insights and other words that relate to this week's vocabulary.

Picture It

Copy this word organizer into your vocabulary journal. Fill in the chart with things you **anticipate**.

anticipate
my next birthday

Copy this word web into your vocabulary journal. Fill in the word web with different words that describe a **surface**.

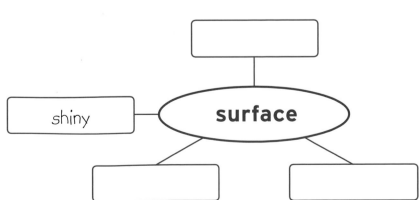

shiny — **surface**

195

Use Fix-Up Strategies

FIX-UP STRATEGIES help you when you get stuck on a word.

When you get stuck on a word, try different strategies to help you figure it out.

TURN AND TALK Listen as your teacher reads from *Into the Volcano* and models how to use fix-up strategies. Then discuss answers to these questions.

- Did you hear any word in the text that you did not understand?

- What fix-up strategy could you use to help you understand?

TAKE IT WITH YOU Using fix-up strategies can help you understand difficult words in what you read. As you read other texts, try to choose the best fix-up strategy to help you understand what you read.

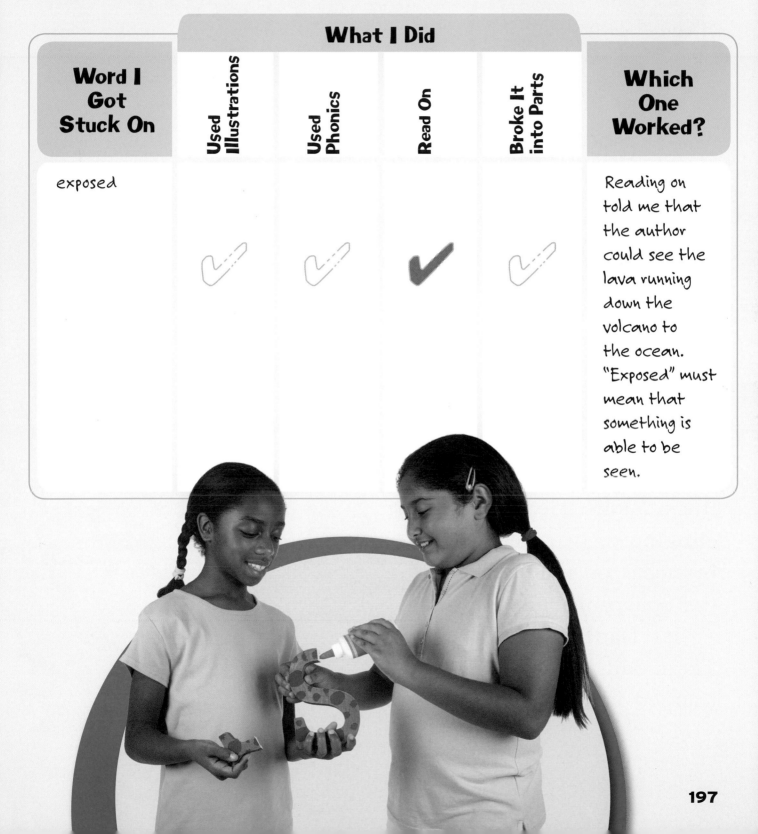

Word I Got Stuck On	What I Did				Which One Worked?
	Used Illustrations	Used Phonics	Read On	Broke It into Parts	
exposed	✓	✓	✔	✓	Reading on told me that the author could see the lava running down the volcano to the ocean. "Exposed" must mean that something is able to be seen.

DANGER LURKS Underground

by Mike Graf

Erica and Tim ran to Coal Street. They saw rough, broken pavement where smooth sidewalks had once been. They came to the edge of a huge, steaming sinkhole. The smoke from the hole smelled like rotten eggs. The weak ground had collapsed. About 50 feet below, the orange bottom burned and crackled like hot coals.

Tim peered through the thick smoke. He saw someone clinging to two tree branches on the side of the collapsing hole.

"It's Dad!" Tim yelled. Their dad, a fire chief, was trapped in the sinkhole.

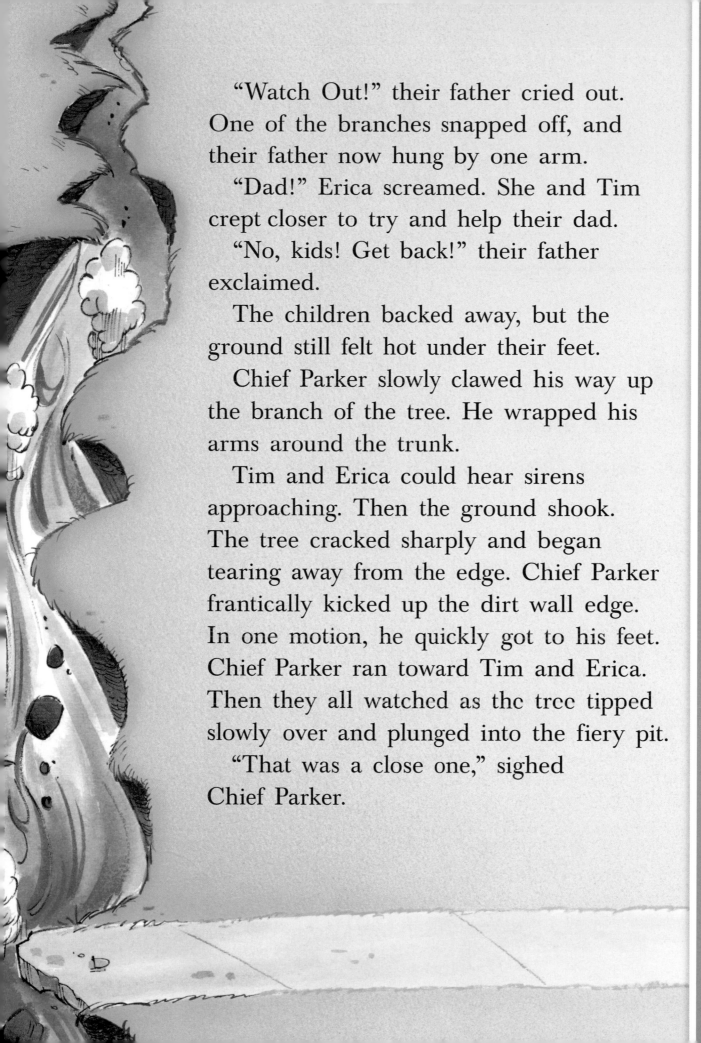

"Watch Out!" their father cried out. One of the branches snapped off, and their father now hung by one arm.

"Dad!" Erica screamed. She and Tim crept closer to try and help their dad.

"No, kids! Get back!" their father exclaimed.

The children backed away, but the ground still felt hot under their feet.

Chief Parker slowly clawed his way up the branch of the tree. He wrapped his arms around the trunk.

Tim and Erica could hear sirens approaching. Then the ground shook. The tree cracked sharply and began tearing away from the edge. Chief Parker frantically kicked up the dirt wall edge. In one motion, he quickly got to his feet. Chief Parker ran toward Tim and Erica. Then they all watched as the tree tipped slowly over and plunged into the fiery pit.

"That was a close one," sighed Chief Parker.

ASK A SCIENTIST!

Welcome to **Ask a Scientist!** Our guest today is Dr. Magma, a seismologist. She studies earthquakes and their effects.

Q: What causes an earthquake?

A: The Earth's outer surface is broken into several parts. These parts are called plates. They float on top of fluid inside the Earth. The movement between plates is not smooth. Plates rub up against each other and cause rough collisions. The plates push and shove each other around. This action causes earthquakes.

Q: How long does an earthquake last?

A: Most earthquakes last only a brief amount of time. Even big ones are often short and last less than one minute. Still, they affect large areas of land.

Synonyms and Antonyms

Activity One

About Synonyms and Antonyms

Synonyms are words that have the same or almost the same meaning. Antonyms are words that are opposite in meaning. Here are examples of synonym pairs: *woods* and *forest*, *happy* and *delighted*, *kinds* and *types*. Here are some antonym pairs: *burn* and *freeze*, *leave* and *arrive*, *remember* and *forget*. As your teacher reads the selection, read along and look for pairs of words that are synonyms and antonyms.

Synonyms and Antonyms in Context

With a partner, read back through *Ask a Scientist!* to find synonym pairs and antonym pairs. Write a list of the words you find.

Activity Two

Explore Words Together

Work with a partner and take turns choosing a word from the list on the right. Work together to write a synonym and an antonym for each word.

move	break
tiny	fast
rough	noisy

Activity Three

Explore Words in Writing

Write sentences about what it would be like to experience an earthquake. Be sure to include pairs of synonyms and antonyms. Have a partner find the synonyms and antonyms.

Yellowstone National Park: *Land of Wonders*

by Marjorie Murray

Yellowstone National Park

Yellowstone Lake

In northwestern Wyoming, you will discover an unusual but wonderful place. It is Yellowstone National Park.

The earth at Yellowstone changes right before your eyes. It rumbles, bubbles, and gushes around the clock. Geysers send boiling water soaring into the air. Colorful canyons, hot springs, and bubbling mud pots cover the land. You might even feel a small earthquake. Thousands of earthquakes happen within the park every year. Luckily, they leave no damage to repair. Yellowstone is always on the move!

What words describing Yellowstone were difficult to understand? How did you figure them out?

How Was Yellowstone Formed?

Over millions of years, many volcanoes erupted in this area. Some of the volcanoes in the park were huge. They would make Hawaii's Kilauea seem tiny. The last eruption was more than 600,000 years ago. It shaped the land into what we see today.

What strategies could you use to figure out the meaning of "erupted"?

The volcano shook the earth for thousands of miles. Huge amounts of ash blasted into the sky. Some of this ancient ash can still be found in places far from Yellowstone. It has been found in Iowa, Louisiana, and California!

Yellowstone is actually the crater on top of that volcano. This part of a volcano is called a *caldera*. The Yellowstone caldera is about 35 miles wide and 50 miles long. Today you can still see the walls of the enormous pit.

Yellowstone Cliffs

Geyser Country

The same volcanic forces are still active beneath Yellowstone's surface today. These forces produce geysers. A geyser is a hot spring that shoots water high into the air. Yellowstone has more than 300 geysers. That's more than any other place in the world!

The conditions at Yellowstone are just right for creating these amazing events. First, rain and snow fall on the ground. The water trickles down through cracks in the rock. It collects in pools below ground.

Next, deep below the surface, liquid rock called *magma*, heats the water. When the water boils, it rises back up through the cracks. Rock and ash fall into the cracks and block the path of the water. This creates pressure.

Finally, the very hot water makes its way to the surface. The pressure drops. Then boiling water and steam shoot high into the air as a geyser.

Read, Cover, Remember, Retell Technique With a partner, take turns reading as much text as you can cover with your hand. Then cover up what you read and retell the information to your partner.

Diagram of a Geyser

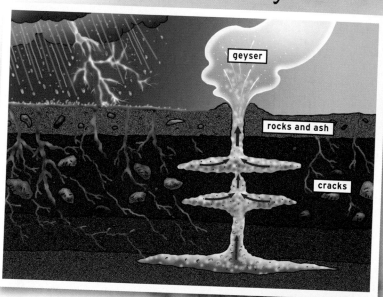

geyser

rocks and ash

cracks

What strategies could help you understand the meaning of "magma"?

Visiting the Park

People come from near and far to see the amazing natural attractions at Yellowstone. Here are some of the park's must-see attractions.

Old Faithful This geyser erupts about every hour and a half. The water shoots up more than 100 feet into the air. That's as high as a ten-story building! The water is over 200 degrees Fahrenheit.

Grand Canyon of the Yellowstone It took thousands of years to form this canyon. The water from melting glaciers carved out the earth's crust. The canyon is 800 to 1200 feet deep. Today a river flows at the bottom of the canyon and forms several beautiful waterfalls.

Lower Falls There are more than forty waterfalls in Yellowstone. The Lower Falls is the tallest waterfall in the park. It is 308 feet high.

What is a canyon? How does reading on help you to understand what it means?

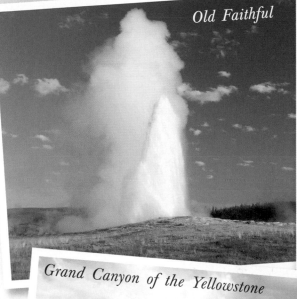

Old Faithful

Grand Canyon of the Yellowstone

Lower Falls

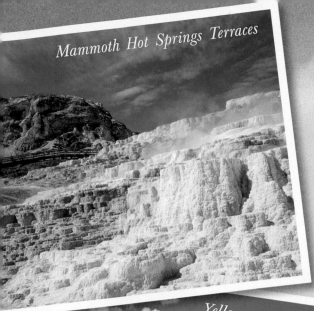
Mammoth Hot Springs Terraces

Yellowstone Lake

Mammoth Hot Springs Terraces How would you like to look at a stairway made of a rock called limestone? The water from hot springs spills over the limestone steps.

Yellowstone Lake Yellowstone Lake is the largest natural mountain lake in the United States. It is 20 miles long and 14 miles wide.

Bubbling Mud Pots Have you ever smelled rotten eggs? That's what it smells like here. But don't let that keep you away. The mud pots are an amazing sight. You can watch acid boil rocks right before your eyes. The result is natural pots of bubbling mud.

What strategies could you use to figure out the meaning of "limestone"?

Fast Fact

Yellowstone is the oldest national park in the United States. In 1872, President Ulysses S. Grant signed a law to make Yellowstone a public park. This means the land can never be bought or changed. He wanted people to enjoy the wonders of the park forever.

Bubbling Mud Pots

Think and Respond

Reflect and Write

- You and your partner have read and retold sections of *Yellowstone National Park*. Discuss with your partner your retellings.

- Choose a page from the reading. On one side of an index card, write a word or a sentence that you had trouble understanding. On the other side, write a strategy that can help you understand each item.

Synonyms and Antonyms in Context

Search through *Yellowstone National Park: Land of Wonders* to find pairs of words that are synonyms or antonyms. Make a list of your word pairs and compare them with a partner's.

Turn and Talk

USE FIX-UP STRATEGIES

Discuss with a partner how fix-up strategies help you as you read.

- What are fix-up strategies?

With a partner, read page 202 again. Discuss which words you found difficult to read. Talk with a partner about the fix-up strategies you can use.

Critical Thinking

With a partner, discuss how Yellowstone National Park was formed. Then talk about the different sights at Yellowstone. Make a list of ways the earth is moving and changing at Yellowstone. Then answer these questions.

- How does the history of the land affect Yellowstone today?

- Why do you think millions of people visit Yellowstone?

Danger, Sinkholes!

A sinkhole makes a big pit.

An **earthquake** is not the only event that can shake things up! Sinkholes also change Earth's surface. Sinkholes form when water underground causes the ground above to collapse. This creates a pit. People have to be **alert** when a sinkhole occurs. Sinkholes can **demolish** roads. They can cause a **landslide**. Sinkholes are difficult to **repair**.

Lake Jackson drained into a sinkhole in 1999.

Lake Jackson in Florida was a large, healthy lake. Then a sinkhole opened beneath the lake. The lake drained like a tub. Fish and alligators spun around in a whirlpool. Soon everything in the lake disappeared down the hole!

Structured Vocabulary Discussion

Answer each of the following questions. Explain each answer.

- Would you **repair** a new book or a broken toy?

- When do you feel **alert**?

- Would you more likely see a **landslide** near a cliff or in the ocean?

Throughout the week, add to your vocabulary journal entries. Record new insights and other words that relate to this week's vocabulary.

Picture It

Copy this word organizer into your vocabulary journal. Give examples of action words that mean about the same as **repair**.

repair

put back together			

Copy the following word web into your vocabulary journal. Fill in the circles with things that an **earthquake** does.

destroys roads

earthquake

Genre
Poem

Black Sand Beach

by John Andrews

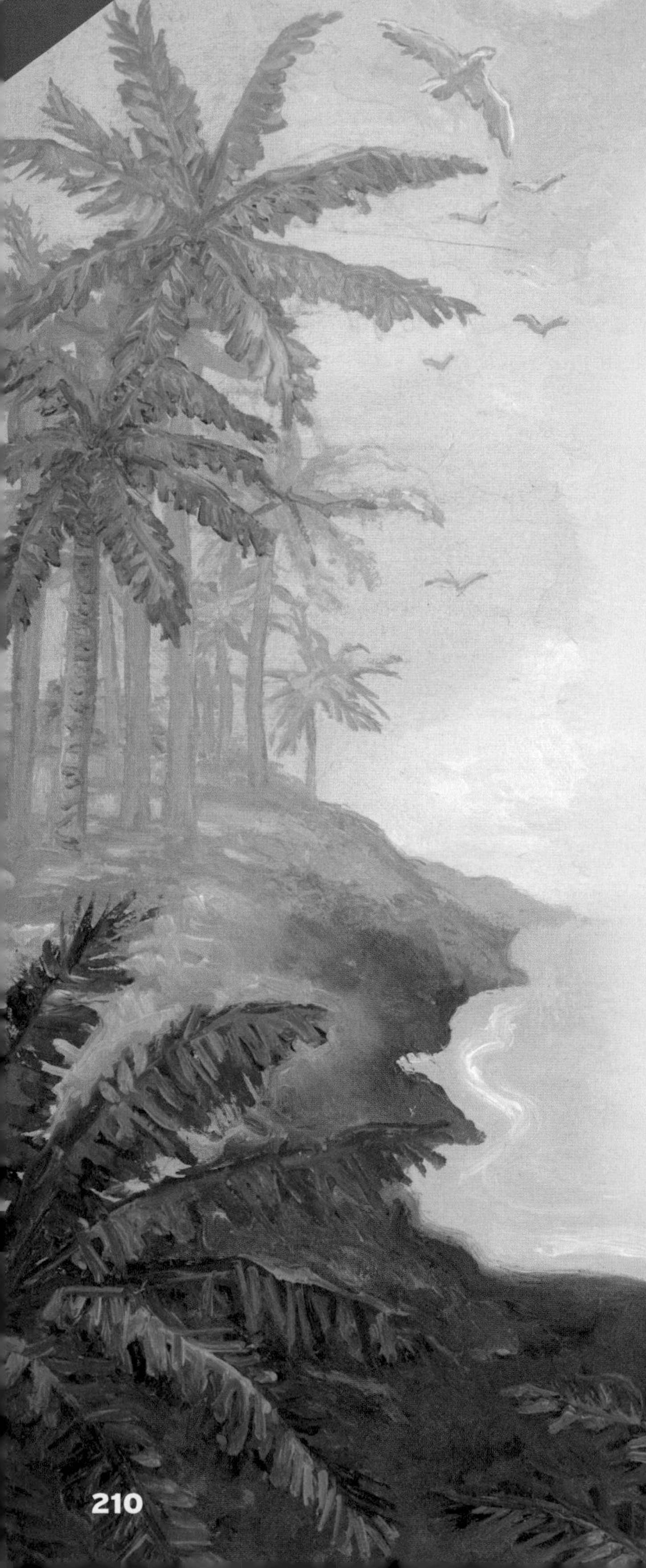

I kick off my flip-flops
and feel the black sand–
so hot on my feet,
and in my tanned hand.

As the birds fly above,
I hear their wings flap.
Do they wonder how
this beach became black?

With each wave that crashes
and smashes the shore,
I think of volcanoes
and Earth's fiery core.

The tension was building,
magma pushed to the top.
The pressure was great,
and then suddenly, pop!

Were the fish all alert
when the lava poured down?
Did they hear a soft fizzle
as each ember drowned?

The sizzling lava,
that cooled over time
created this beach
on which we recline.

A Ten-Year-Old HERO

Tilly Smith reads a poem at a memorial service on the first anniversary of the 2004 tsunami.

In December 2004, 10-year-old Tilly Smith was on vacation with her parents. They were at a beach in Thailand. Tilly saw the calm waters next to the beach begin to bubble and foam. She was suddenly very worried. Other people stopped to watch. They did not know what was happening. But Tilly knew. She had studied this at school. Earthquakes under the ocean cause tsunamis. A tsunami is a series of huge waves.

Tilly told her parents a tsunami was bound for the beach. They told the others to dash for the hotel. A few minutes later, the tsunami hit. The people watched the water pound the shore from the hotel. Everyone was safe. If people had stayed on the beach, they would have drowned. Thanks to Tilly, everyone on that beach was safe.

Multiple-Meaning Words

Activity One

About Multiple-Meaning Words

Some words have more than one meaning. For example, a *bat* is something you use to hit a baseball. A *bat* is also an animal that can fly. As your teacher reads *A Ten-Year-Old Hero*, listen for multiple-meaning words and how they are used. Here are examples of multiple meaning words: *back*, *kind*, *present*, *fault*, *block*, *pitcher*.

Multiple-Meaning Words in Context

With a small group, read *A Ten-Year-Old Hero*. Find each word that has more than one meaning, and make a list. Discuss how each word is used in the passage. Then give a second meaning for the word.

Activity Two

Explore Words Together

Work with a partner to write two sentences for each word on the right. Use a different meaning for the word in each sentence. Share your sentences with the class.

leaves	rose
mind	model
crush	spot

Tidal waves wash through Sri Lanka.

Activity Three

Explore Words in Writing

Write two sentences that each use a different multiple-meaning word from Activity One or Two. Leave a blank space for the multiple-meaning word. Exchange sentences with a partner and fill in the blanks with the correct multiple-meaning word.

It's Not My Fault!

by Mark Donaldson

María Montez was drawing imaginary fault lines on the back of her notebook. Her class was studying earthquakes . . . again! María put her hand over her mouth to cover up a big yawn. She looked out the window. She stared at the mountains and sighed. Her town was practically on top of the San Andreas Fault line. Everyone seemed to talk about it every single minute.

Even at home, María's parents were always talking about earthquakes. They wanted to move to a new house. They wanted to find one that was built on granite rock. That way, it would be on firm ground. "Earthquakes find their way into everything," María thought.

What picture do you have in your mind of Maria?

BRRRING! The bell rang for recess. María ran outside. She was ready for a soccer game.

"María!" called out her friend Stella. "Come and play on our side!"

After kickoff, María got the ball. She raced up the field and headed for the goal. Then Tanya Jackson, the soccer star, came out of nowhere.

What picture of the soccer game do you have in your mind when the ground begins to tremble?

Tanya knocked the ball away from María and headed back down the field.

I wish, María thought, *I wish we'd have an earthquake! Just a teeny, tiny one to keep Tanya from scoring.*

Just then, Tanya's legs wobbled. The ground underneath her was trembling. There was a soft rumbling noise. María stole the ball and scored a goal.

"We've been studying earthquakes for two weeks now," said Mrs. Lee after recess. "It's time for a pop quiz."

María was worried. Then she smiled. She knew how to make earthquakes happen!

It was time for another one. María closed her eyes. *I wish for a medium-sized earthquake,* she thought.

Suddenly, the classroom floor rolled like waves on the ocean. The ceiling cracked and paint crackled. The fire alarm blared.

"Drop, cover, and hold on!" Mrs. Lee yelled. "Crawl to the inside wall!"

Two-Word Technique Write down two words that reflect your thoughts about each page. Discuss them with your partner.

How does this passage help you create a mental image of an earthquake?

As quickly as it had begun, the quake was over. María thought she had caused another earthquake. This one was a little

Do the events on this page change the mental image you have of Maria? Explain.

scary. Her hands were sweating and her knees were shaking worse than the Earth had!

Moments later, the whole school was shaking again, but not from an earthquake. She looked out the window and saw an avalanche of rock and dirt heading toward the school.

"Landslide!" Mrs. Lee yelled.

Everyone started to run, screaming, out of the building. But the landslide was too fast. It kept coming closer and closer. It was going to demolish the school.

"Help!" screamed María. "HELP!"

"María," said Mrs. Lee, shaking her shoulder. "Wake up. You dozed off. I guess earthquakes aren't exciting enough for you."

María shook her head and opened her eyes. She was back in her classroom.

"Oh, Mrs. Lee," she said. "We had three earthquakes! I made them happen. And then the earthquakes caused a landslide. We were all about to be crushed!"

How has Maria's story changed the mental image you have about earthquakes?

"I think you just had a bad dream during your little nap," said Mrs. Lee. "Earthquakes are very dangerous. That's why we spend so much time learning about them."

"I know that now," María sighed. "And I'm glad that they're not my fault! Earthquakes are a nightmare."

Just as soon as the words were out of María's mouth, the Earth began to shake.

Think and Respond

Reflect and Write

- You and your partner have read *It's Not My Fault!* and written two words about each page. Discuss your words and your thoughts.

- On one side of an index card write your favorite mental image from the story. On the other side, write the words that helped you create the image.

Multiple-Meaning Words in Context

Search through *It's Not My Fault!* to find words that can have more than one meaning. Write one sentence for each meaning of the words you find.

Turn and Talk

CREATE IMAGES

Discuss with a partner what you have learned about creating mental images as you read.

- How does creating mental images help you understand what you read?

Reread page 216 with a partner. Then write a list of mental images you had as you read.

Critical Thinking

With a partner, discuss what happened in the story after each earthquake. Make a list of words that describe an earthquake. Then answer these questions.

- How does Maria's attitude toward earthquakes change? Why do her feelings change?

- How do you feel about earthquakes after reading the story?

THEME 8

Predicting Nature's Hazards

Contents

Modeled Reading

Shared Reading

Interactive Reading

THE LLAMA'S SECRET

by Argentina Palacios

illustrated by Charles Reasoner

A PERUVIAN LEGEND

Appreciative Listening

Appreciative listening means listening for particular words and phrases that you enjoy hearing. Listen to the focus questions your teacher will read to you.

Animal Smarts

What Animals Know

Some animals know when danger is near. In 2004, a giant wave called a *tsunami* crashed into parts of Asia. Some people in the area say that before the wave came, animals showed **concern**. Elephants ran to high ground. Dogs ran, too. Birds and bats took **flight**. Perhaps they did this to get away from danger.

How Do They Know?

How do animals know when trouble is on the way? **Curiosity** makes people try to learn the answer. Some people believe animals feel changes in the air before an earthquake. They may also feel movements in the ground. However they do it, animals show **caution** when danger is near. This can be a **warning** to people!

Structured Vocabulary Discussion

Work with a partner to complete these sentences about your vocabulary words.

_____ and _____ are *similar* because both describe how people act when danger is near.

_____ and _____ are *different*. One is a way for someone to know danger ahead of time. The other is a way that someone might escape danger.

> Throughout the week, add to your vocabulary journal entries. Record new insights and other words that relate to this week's vocabulary.

Picture It

Copy this word web into your vocabulary journal. In each circle, write a kind of **warning** that you have heard or given.

warning

car horn

Copy these word charts into your vocabulary journal. In the first row of boxes, write words that are related to **caution**. In the second row, write ways to show **caution**.

caution

careful		

go slowly		

225

Comprehension Strategy

Determine Importance

Think about the most **IMPORTANT** ideas.

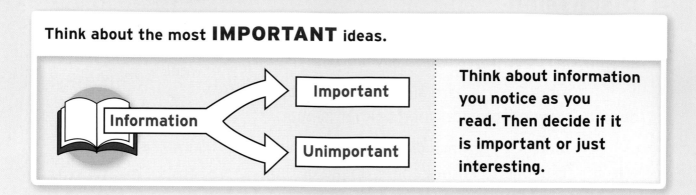

Think about information you notice as you read. Then decide if it is important or just interesting.

TURN AND TALK Listen as your teacher reads from *The Llama's Secret* and models how to determine importance. Then discuss with a partner answers to these questions.

- What is the most important idea from this passage?

- How do you determine what is most important and what is not?

TAKE IT WITH YOU Determining the importance of information helps you understand and remember important ideas. When you read, look for the important information. Use a chart like the one below to help you decide what is important as you read.

Information That I Noticed	Important?	Explain Your Thinking
The llama tells the man how to escape the flood. He is to go to the mountain and take enough food for five days.	☑ **Important!** ☐ **Unimportant but Interesting**	The llama's words will tell the man how to stay alive in the flood. This is important information.
The wife is spinning cloth from llama's wool.	☐ **Important!** ☑ **Unimportant but Interesting**	This is interesting because I didn't know llamas' wool could be used for cloth. The information is unimportant compared to escaping the flood.

On Hurricane Watch

by Michelle Sale

June 5 12:00 P.M.

Hurricane season began last week. My observation log will record the weather over the season. For example, today it is raining. I hear thunder and see lightning, too. Is this thunderstorm coming ahead of a hurricane? I will watch to see what happens. Weather radar equipment will help me track where the storms are going.

June 6 4:00 P.M.

A large weather system is moving over the Atlantic Ocean. It is 100 miles south of Florida. Here, in Palm Beach, it is sunny. But on the weather maps, winds seem to be moving in a circle over the sea. The winds are one warning a hurricane might be coming.

June 8 3:00 P.M.

The weather system I noticed a few days ago is moving toward Florida. Everyone in Palm Beach had hoped the system would move away from land. But the storm turned toward us and is getting stronger all the time.

June 9   9:30 A.M.

It's raining very hard in Miami, south of here. This morning, wind blew my umbrella out of my hands! Winds are blowing at 30 miles an hour. (This is about as fast as a slow-moving car.) The winds move counterclockwise. That means this storm is a tropical depression.

June 10   2:15 P.M.

This storm is moving very fast. Trees near my office bend and sway from the strong winds. Our weather radar says the winds are blowing almost 70 mph. (This is as fast as a car drives on the highway.) That means this system is a tropical storm. We will give it a name from our storm list. Its name will be George. We must warn people to use caution outside.

June 11   6:30 A.M.

George became a hurricane this morning. Wind speeds reached 105 mph. Half the homes in Florida have lost power. Winds knocked down two trees near our own weather center. Garbage and papers are all over the ground. Fortunately, I think we were able to warn people in time!

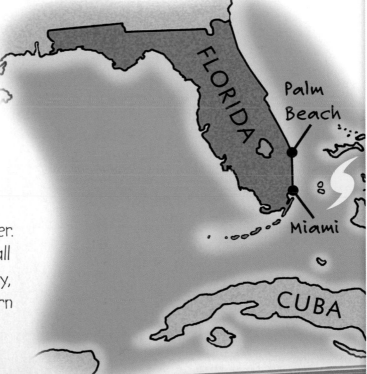

Ask A Weather Expert

Mary Ann Clary has been a TV reporter in Baton Rouge, Louisiana. Her viewers always liked to hear her descriptions of weather. Here she answers some questions about reporting wild weather.

What is it like to report weather in your area?

Sometimes we have very frightening weather. There are thunderstorms, tornadoes, hurricanes, and flooding. Sometimes we even get snow or ice. To sum it up, I'm busy reporting the changes!

Can you tell about one bad storm you have seen?

Hurricane Lili, in 2002, was a bad storm. We thought it would be a Category 5 hurricane, the strongest kind. However, it turned into a Category 1 storm. That kind of storm is not as dangerous. Hurricane Lili still damaged many homes and businesses.

What is the strangest thing you have seen on the job?

Once lightning hit our station and came through a vent into the newsroom. Our director's hair stood straight up! He threw himself under a table. Luckily, he was not hurt. We all laughed! It was quite a scene!

Homonyms

Activity One

About Homonyms

Homonyms are words that sound the same but have different spellings and meanings. Here is a list of homonyms you might know: *be, bee; see, sea; sight, site; blew, blue; eight, ate; know, no.* As your teacher reads the *Ask A Weather Expert*, listen for words that are homonyms.

THE WEATHER NEWS TEAM

Homonyms in Context

Read *Ask A Weather Expert* with a partner. Make a list of the homonym pairs you find. Compare your list with another partner team's list. Together, talk about the different meanings of the words in each pair.

Activity Two

plain	plane
road	rode
week	weak

Explore Words Together

Work with a partner. Find meanings for the words in each homonym pair in the box. Be ready to share your meanings with the rest of the class.

Activity Three

Explore Words in Writing

Work with a partner to write a paragraph about weather. Use two homonym pairs from Activity One or Two. Be sure your sentences show the different meanings of the homonyms.

The Storm Chasers

by Ann Weil

"Hurry, or we'll be late for the game!"

Joel grabbed his mitt with one hand and his baseball cap in the other. His brother Patrick was waiting for him. Patrick did not like to be late.

"Don't forget your jackets," said their mom. "It's looking a bit stormy."

The sky was mostly blue with only a few clouds in it. Still, the boys took their jackets off the hooks by the door. Their mother knew weather better than almost anyone except maybe their father. Their parents worked together as storm chasers. Their job was to track storms, measure how strong they were, and take photographs and videos.

What important information do you learn about Joel and Patrick's family?

"Your father will meet us at the game," she said. "He has to buy some new equipment for the van."

"Did something break?" asked Joel.

"No," said Mom, "but we need a new anemometer (ane-MOM-eat-er). That's the tool we use to measure wind speed. A new one will be more accurate." Patrick knew that having the best equipment gave his parents an advantage in their work.

232

By the time they got to the ball field, the sky was dark with clouds. Patrick saw a flash of lightning. It began to rain as the boys got out of the car. They ran over to their coach who was packing up the sports equipment. "Sorry, boys," the coach told them. "The game is cancelled. I just heard on the radio that there's a tornado watch."

Just then Dad's van pulled into the parking lot.

"Can we check out the storm?" asked Joel.

"Sure," said Mom. "I'll leave our car here and pick it up later." They all piled into the van and drove off toward the storm.

"I hope we see a tornado," said Joel.

What information on this page is important for you to understand the story so far?

Patrick wasn't so sure that he wanted to see a tornado, at least not close up. He knew how dangerous a tornado could be. But he trusted his parents to keep him safe.

"Look!" said Mom, pointing through the window at a cloud with a strange green color. Another cloud near it began to spin. "Here it comes," said Mom as they saw a tornado form in the sky.

"Let's look for cover," said Dad as he started to brake. The van stopped next to an old farmhouse.

"Why are we here?" asked Joel.

"Mom and I know the people who live here. We sometimes use their basement to escape a bad storm," said Dad. "You'll be safe here. I'm going to try to get some good video of this twister. I'll be back for you in an hour."

"Good luck!" Mom called.

Say Something Technique Take turns reading a section of text, covering it up, and then saying something about it to your partner. You may say any thought or idea that the text brings to your mind.

Is what Mom says in the last paragraph an important detail in the story? Why do you think so?

Patrick was the first into the cellar. All he could hear was the roar of the wind. He was scared.

"Don't worry," said his mother. "We'll be fine down here."

"But what about Dad?" said Joel.

Mom smiled. "Your father knows what he's doing. He'll be back soon with some great video."

After a few minutes, Patrick took a piece of bubble gum from his pocket and blew a big bubble. He wasn't scared anymore. Now he was just bored.

Joel played a game with his blue baseball cap. He threw it up toward the ceiling. Then he tried to catch it on his head. "Can we go now?" he asked, finally.

What is important information on this page? What is interesting but unimportant? Explain.

Tornado Alley

The United States has more tornadoes than other countries, and most of these deadly storms occur in "Tornado Alley." This region may see thousands of tornadoes in one year. Oklahoma and Texas have more tornadoes than any other states.

Mom opened the cellar door and looked out. "All clear," she said. They climbed out of the cellar just as Dad pulled in next to the farmhouse.

What is the most important event in this story? What makes you think it is important?

"I got it!" Dad said in an excited voice. They all piled into the back of the van to watch the video. The van was full of equipment used to track and record storms. Dad even had a special two-way radio in the van. That way he could talk to other storm chasers while he was on the road.

"Look, you can see the shape of the tornado," said Dad, pointing to the tornado on the monitor. "I already e-mailed this to the local news station. The national news may use it tonight, too."

That evening, the boys watched the local news. The tornado was the big story. "They're showing Dad's video again," said Joel. Patrick was glad to see a tornado up close again, so long as it was on TV.

Think and Respond

Reflect and Write

- You and your partner have read *The Storm Chasers* and said something about it. Discuss your thoughts and ideas with your partner.

- On one side of an index card, write a piece of important information that you noticed in the story. On the other side, write why you decided it is important.

Homonyms in Context

Search through *The Storm Chasers* to find pairs of words that are homonyms. Make a list of your word pairs and compare them with a partner's.

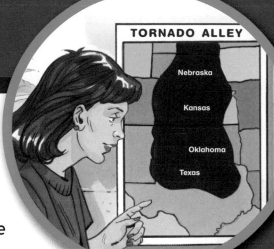

Turn and Talk

DETERMINE IMPORTANCE

Discuss with a partner what you have learned so far about how to determine importance.

- How do you determine the importance of ideas and details as you read?

With a partner, look back at page 233. Discuss what information is important and what information is interesting but not important. Explain your thinking.

Critical Thinking

With a partner, discuss what you know about tornadoes. Look back at *The Storm Chasers*. Write what you learn from the story about tornadoes. Then answer these questions.

- Do you think the parents in the story have dangerous jobs? Why or why not?

- Why is it important for people to predict dangerous weather?

Vocabulary

Weather Tips
...In the Air!

1 Pilot:
Hello, Air Traffic Control. This is Flight D34 to Atlanta, Georgia. We've been checking the weather **forecast** for today. We need to **evaluate** our flight path.

2 Air Traffic Controller:
Roger, Flight D34. The most **accurate** forecast predicts storms throughout the Midwest. Look for high winds and rain over Kansas and Oklahoma.

3 Pilot:
Would it be to our **advantage** to fly over Texas to avoid storms? Would clouds or other weather make this a bumpy ride?

4 Controller:
No, weather looks clear over Texas. Air traffic controllers in Dallas will come to your **aid** if storms move there. Have a good flight!

238

Structured Vocabulary Discussion

When your teacher says a vocabulary word, each person in your small group will take turns saying the first word that comes to mind. When your teacher says "Stop," the last person who spoke will explain how that word is related to the vocabulary word.

Throughout the week, add to your vocabulary journal entries. Record new insights and other words that relate to this week's vocabulary.

Picture It

Copy this chart into your vocabulary journal. Fill in the chart with activities for which it helps to be **accurate**.

accurate
Math homework

Copy this word wheel into your vocabulary journal. Fill in the top with items that would **aid** you in a snowstorm. Fill in the bottom with items that would not **aid** you in a snowstorm.

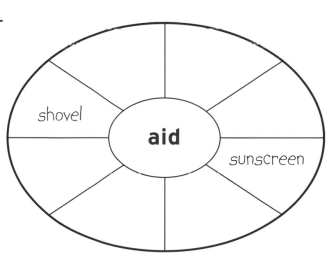

shovel

aid

sunscreen

Foggy Morning at Mt. Pleasant

by Lorraine Sintetos

Morning sun warmed the chilled lake.

Then our valley filled with fog

as far as the eye could see.

Now, above the fog, Mt. Pleasant rises

like an island above the sea,

welcoming and proud.

High in the sky the sun begins
to burn the A.M. mist,
turning it to clouds.

Pine needles are an aid to the sun,
shredding the last bits of fog to wisps.
Morning is done.

Science Experiment: Twister in a Jar

A tornado is a powerful storm with winds shaped like a funnel. This experiment shows how a tornado is shaped. Try doing the experiment with friends or a family member!

You will need:

- a jar with a tight lid, such as a peanut butter jar
- water
- clear liquid soap
- vinegar
- glitter (optional)

Steps:

1. Fill the jar about three quarters full of water.

2. Add a teaspoon of soap and a teaspoon of vinegar.

3. For a sparkling tornado, add glitter!

4. Put the lid on the jar. Make sure it is closed tightly. Shake well.

5. Try swirling the jar in a circle. Do you see a tornado forming?

Word Endings -ed, -ing, and -s

Activity One

About Word Endings -ed, -ing, and -s

The endings -ed, -ing and -s can be added to many words. The ending will change the meaning of the word. Here are examples of words with the endings -ed, -ing, and -s: *walked, tried, pressed, riding, frying, laughing, running, teaches, races, hurries*. As your teacher reads *Twister in a Jar* aloud, listen for words with the endings -ed, -ing, and -s.

Word Endings -ed, -ing, and -s in Context

With a partner, read *Twister in a Jar*. Make a list of words that have the endings -ed, -ing, and -s. Talk about how the ending helps you understand the meaning of each word.

Activity Two

Explore Words Together

Work with a partner to add endings -ed, -ing, and -s to the words on the right. Add as many of the endings to each word as you can.

chew	make
heart	crowd
enjoy	shirt

Activity Three

Explore Words in Writing

Write a short paragraph about a time when you experienced wild weather. Use words with the endings -ed, -ing, and -s. Circle the words with these endings. Share your work with a partner.

WILD WEATHER!

by Margaret Fetty

What's the weather like today? This is probably one of the first questions you ask each morning. The weather often affects what you wear, what you do, and where you go. If it's raining, your picnic at the park will have to wait. Snow means you will need to wear a warm coat, boots, and gloves.

Most of the time, a weather forecast can help you plan. People who forecast weather evaluate weather patterns. Then they predict what the weather will be like. Sometimes Mother Nature sends a surprise, though. The forecast can change quickly, and the weather may get wild. Just how wild can weather get? Let's look at some amazing weather records!

What strategies can help you understand the phrase "Mother Nature"?

WET WEATHER

How wet can one place get?

Take an umbrella when you visit Mount Waialeale (wy-ah-lay-AH-lee), Hawaii. It's the wettest place in the world. It rains there about 350 days a year. About 460 inches of rain fall each year. That's more than an inch every day!

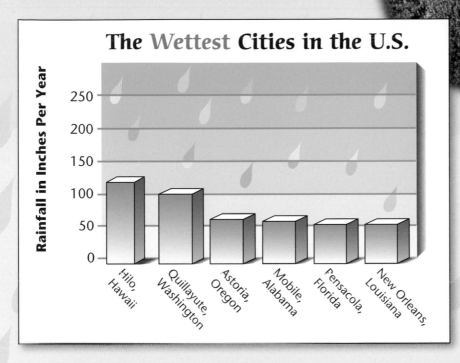

The Wettest Cities in the U.S.

How much rain can fall in one month?

Cherrapunji (chur-a-PUN-gee), India is dry for part of the year. But during the summer monsoon season, it can rain for months without stopping. In July of 1861, cold ocean winds brought 366 inches of rain. More than 1,042 inches of rain fell from August 1860 to July 1861. That's more than 86 feet of rain!

What strategy could you use to help you understand what a *monsoon* is?

COLD WEATHER

How cold can one place get?

Antarctica is covered in ice. The average temperature in Antarctica is −67°F. On July 21, 1983, the temperature reached a new low. It was −129°F!

How much snow can one storm leave behind?

People in Mount Shasta, California remember 1959. Snow fell from February 13–19. After seven days, 189 inches of snow had fallen. Most of the snow fell high up on the mountain, where few people lived. So many people did not know that they had seen a record-breaking storm.

How big can a snowflake get?

Moist air makes big snowflakes. On Jan. 28, 1887, the air must have been really moist in Fort Keogh (KEY-og), Montana. A rancher saw the world's largest snowflake. It measured 15 inches wide and 8 inches thick.

A weather station in Antarctica

Partner Jigsaw Technique Read a section of the article with a partner and write down one fix-up strategy you used. Be prepared to summarize your section and share one fix-up strategy.

Are there any words on this page that are new to you? How can you figure out what they mean?

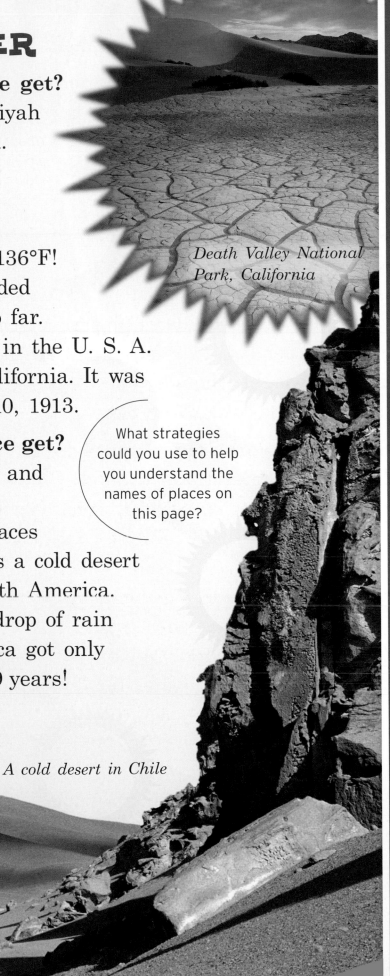

HOT WEATHER

How hot can one place get?

Let's travel to Al Aziziyah (al-a-zee-ZEE-yah), Libya. This desert town is in Northern Africa. On September 13, 1922, the temperature climbed to 136°F! This is the hottest recorded temperature on Earth so far.

The hottest afternoon in the U. S. A. was in Death Valley, California. It was a toasty 134°F on July 10, 1913.

How dry can one place get?

Earth has hot deserts and cold deserts. Hot or cold, deserts are the driest places on Earth. Arica, Chile is a cold desert in the mountains of South America. Arica did not have one drop of rain in 14 years. In fact, Arica got only 0.03 inches of rain in 59 years!

Death Valley National Park, California

What strategies could you use to help you understand the names of places on this page?

A cold desert in Chile

EXTREME WEATHER

How big was the biggest tornado?

The biggest tornado blasted through Hallam, Nebraska on May 22, 2004. This tornado was more than $2\frac{1}{2}$ miles wide.

What strategy could help you if you did not know the meaning of "hailstone"?

Hailstones

How big can a hailstone get?

Aurora, Nebraska, holds the record for the biggest hailstone. The hailstone measured more than 7 inches wide. That's about the size of a soccer ball! The scientists are not sure of its weight, though. The hailstone hit a house and broke into pieces.

What is the worst flood on record?

The Yellow River flows through China. Heavy rain causes it to flood often. The worst flood was in June 1887. Water rushed over the dams and flooded more than 50,000 square miles. Two million people lost their homes.

As you can see, weather gets really wild in some parts of the world. Make sure you are ready if wild weather comes to your area!

Think and Respond

Reflect and Write

- You and your partner have read a section of *Wild Weather!* Discuss the strategies each of you used to figure out any difficult word.

- Write down on an index card difficult words from the selection. On the other side of the index card, write the strategy you used. Find another student pair who read different sections and compare your words and strategies.

Word Endings -*ed*, -*ing*, and -*s* in Context

Search through *Wild Weather!* to find words with the endings -*ed*, -*ing*, or -*s*. With a partner, discuss each word and how its meaning would change without the ending.

Turn and Talk

USE FIX-UP STRATEGIES

Discuss with a partner what you have learned so far about using fix-up strategies.

- What are some strategies you can use to figure out difficult words or ideas?

Choose a word from *Wild Weather!* that you had difficulty understanding. Discuss with a partner what fix-up strategies you could use to figure out the meaning.

Critical Thinking

In a small group, discuss some of the places and records you read about in *Wild Weather!* Talk about other places you know that have unusual weather. Then answer these questions.

- What kind of "wild" weather interests you the most? Why?

- Did any of the weather you read about remind you of your own experiences?

Glossary

Using the Glossary

Like a dictionary, this glossary lists words in alphabetical order. Guide words at the top of each page show you the first and last word on the page. If a word has more than one syllable, the syllables are separated by a dark dot (•). Use the pronunciation key on the bottom of every other page.

Sample

The pronunciation guide shows how to say the word. The accent shows which syllable is stressed.

The part of speech shows how the word is often used.

Each word is broken into syllables.

en•vi•ron•ment (en vī′ rən mənt) *n.* The natural world of climate, soil and living things that affect each other. *The Science Club made posters to show ways to save the* **environment.**

The definition shows what the word means.

The example sentence includes the word in it.

Abbreviations: *adj.* adjective, *adv.* adverb, *conj.* conjunction, *interj.* interjection, *n.* noun, *prep.* preposition, *pron.* pronoun, *v.* verb

ath•lete (ath′ lēt′) *n.* A person who is trained in or is very good at exercises, sports, or games that need strength, speed, or skill. *Babe Ruth was a great* **athlete.**

av•a•lanche (av′ ə lanch′) *n.* A large amount of snow, ice, dirt, or rock that suddenly moves down a mountainside. *The* **avalanche** *covered the small town with snow.*

bi•noc•u•lars (bə näk′ yə lərz) *n.* A tool used to see distant objects, made of two small telescopes. *John James Audubon used* **binoculars** *to watch birds.*

ca•ble (kā′ bəl) *n.* A thick, strong rope or wire. *This* **cable** *helps attach the circus tent to the ground.*

cal•i•co (kal′ i kō′) *adj.* Made from cotton cloth that has a colorful pattern. *Kirsten wore a pink* **calico** *dress.*

can•cel (kan′ səl) *v.* To call off something that has already been arranged. *Coach Babin will* **cancel** *the soccer game if it rains.*

can•yon (kan′ yən) *n.* A deep, narrow valley with steep sides. *We visited a* **canyon** *that had a river running through it.*

cape (kāp) *n.* A sleeveless coat that hangs loosely over the shoulders. *The tour guide wore a* **cape** *from the 1800s.*

cer•e•mo•ny (ser′ ə mō′ nē) *n.* A formal act performed in honor of a special event or occasion. *Michelle gave a speech at the graduation* **ceremony.**

charm·ing (chär´ ming) *adj.* Very pleasing or delightful. *The **charming** prince rode to the ball on his horse.*

col·lapse (kə laps´) *v.* To cave in or fall down suddenly. *The bridge may **collapse** under the weight of the truck.*

com·mand (kə mand´) *v.* To give orders; to direct. *The ringmaster can **command** the lion to jump through a hoop of fire.*

com·pe·ti·tion (käm´ pə tish´ ən) *n.* A contest. *On Field Day, there was a tug-of-war **competition** between the third and fourth graders.*

com·put·er (kəm py$\overline{oo}$t´ ər) *n.* An electronic machine that can store, find, and process information. *Jonathan wrote his science report on the **computer.***

con·tract (kän´ trakt´) *n.* A binding legal agreement between two or more people or companies. *The builder signed a **contract** to build the new elementary school.*

cuff (kuf) *n.* The folded part at the bottom of a sleeve or pant leg. *Jimmy wore jeans with a **cuff** turned up at the bottom.*

dis·crim·i·na·tion (di skrim´ i nā´ shən) *n.* Unfair behavior towards others because of differences. *Mr. Locke faced **discrimination** because of his beliefs.*

e·lec·tron (ē lek´ trän´) *n.* A tiny particle that moves around the center of an atom. *An **electron** has a negative electric charge.*

en·vi·ron·ment (en vī´ rən mənt) *n.* The natural world of climate, soil and living things that affect each other. *The Science Club made posters to show ways to save the **environment.***

e·rupt (ē rupt´) *v.* To burst out suddenly. *The volcano is going to **erupt!***

film (film) *n.* A thin strip of material coated with a special chemical that is used in a camera to take photographs. *Dad's camera ran out of **film** when we were on vacation.*

flood (flud) *n.* A large flow of water onto normally dry land. *The **flood** covered the village with water.*

fun·nel (fu´ nəl) *n.* A hollow cone shape. *Mom used a **funnel** to help her pour the lemonade from the pitcher into a bottle.*

PRONUNCIATION KEY

a	add, map	oi	oil, boy	zh	vision, pleasure
ā	ace, rate	ou	pout, now	ə	the schwa, an
â(r)	care, air	∞	took, full		unstressed vowel
ä	palm, father	$\overline{oo}$	pool, food		representing the
e	end, pet	u	up, done		sound spelled
ē	equal, tree	ʉ	her, sir,		*a* in *above*
i	it, give		burn, word		*e* in *sicken*
ī	ice, write	y$\overline{oo}$	fuse, few		*i* in *possible*
o	odd, hot	z	zest, wise		*o* in *melon*
ō	open, so				*u* in *circus*
ô	order, jaw				

guilt·y (gil′ tē) *adj.* Having committed a crime. *The jury decided that the person was **guilty.***

hail·stone (hāl′ stōn′) *n.* A piece or lump of compacted snow and ice. *After the storm, Josh found a giant **hailstone** in his backyard.*

he·li·cop·ter (hel′ i käp′ tər) *n.* An aircraft powered by large, spinning blades on its top. *A **helicopter** does not need a runway to take off or land.*

hum·ble (hum′ bəl) *adj.* Not too proud. *The **humble** professor accepted the Nobel Peace Prize.*

jazz (jaz) *n.* A type of American music marked by a strong rhythm and musicians that sometimes make up their own tunes. ***Jazz** is very popular in New Orleans.*

lan·tern (lan′ tərn) *n.* A protective case that lets the light inside shine through. *Charlotte made a paper **lantern** in art class this morning.*

la·va (lä′ və) *n.* Hot, liquid rock that flows out of a volcano. ***Lava** poured out of Mount Vesuvius.*

lo·cal (lō′ kəl) *adj.* Near, or having to do with a particular place. *Every morning, Grandpa reads the **local** newspaper.*

men·tal (men′ təl) *adj.* Having to do with the mind. *The Quiz Bowl tests your **mental** skills.*

mi·grate (mī′ grāt′) *v.* To move from one place to another. *Every spring, the monarch butterflies **migrate** north toward Canada.*

mu·ral (myoor′ əl) *n.* A painting on a wall or ceiling. *The community painted a **mural** on the wall of the new recreation center.*

mu·si·cian (myoo zi′ shən) *n.* Someone who plays an instrument or sings. *We need another **musician** for our band.*

mut·ter (mu′ tər) *v.* To mumble or speak in a low voice with the lips partly closed. *Mother said, "Don't **mutter** at the table."*

nec·tar (nek′ tər) *n.* A sweet liquid found in flowers. *Hummingbirds drink **nectar.***

ner·vous (nʉr′ vəs) *adj.* Easily excited; jumpy; uneasy. *Abigail was **nervous** when she had to speak in front of her class.*

numb (num) *adj.* Unable to feel anything or to move easily. *Cassie's fingers were **numb** from the cold.*

O·lym·pics (ō lim′ piks) *n.* An international athletic competition held in different cities in winter or summer every two years. *The modern **Olympics** are modeled after an ancient Greek festival.*

or·ches·tra (ôr′ kes trə) *n.* A group of musicians who play their instruments together. *Mrs. Smith plays the violin in an **orchestra.***

pass·port (pas´ pôrt´) *n.* A government document that shows what country someone is from and that lets the person travel to and from other countries. *I need a **passport** to travel overseas during my vacation next summer.*

pos·ture (päs´ chər) *n.* The position of the body. *The ballerina's **posture** was graceful and delicate.*

Pot·latch (pät´ lach´) *n.* A ceremonial feast of Native Americans in the Northwest in which the host presents gifts to the guests. *A **Potlatch** ceremony usually lasts for several days.*

pris·m (priz´ əm) *n.* A clear object that separates white light into different colors. *Cecily's **prism** hung in the window and made a rainbow design on her curtains.*

pump (pump) *n.* A machine that pushes liquid or gas from one place or container into another. *Anthony inflated his bicycle tire with a **pump.***

ra·dar (rā´ där´) *n.* A device that sends out radio waves to find the place or features of distant objects. *The captain used **radar** to find the submarine.*

re·cline (rē klīn´) *v.* To lean back or lie down. *That chair has a button to make it **recline.***

re·sour·ces (rē´ sôr´ sez) *n.* Supplies or materials ready for use, such as money, property, oil, or air. *We must protect our natural **resources.***

se·vere (sə vir´) *adj.* Strict, harsh, or serious. *The weather man predicts a **severe** thunderstorm.*

so·lar (sō´ lər) *adj.* Having to do with the sun. *A **solar** eclipse happens when the moon moves between the sun and Earth.*

trum·pet (trum´ pit) *n.* A musical instrument shaped like a horn. *Chris practices his **trumpet** every day for 30 minutes.*

wind·mill (wind´ mil´) *n.* A machine that uses wind power to grind grain, pump water, or make electricity. *Farmer Don grinds grain into flour at the **windmill.***

wreath (rēth) *n.* Flowers, leaves, or branches that are twisted and tied together in a circle. *Shaneka made a **wreath** of daisies to wear in her hair.*

PRONUNCIATION KEY

a	add, map	oi	oil, boy	zh	vision, pleasure
ā	ace, rate	ou	pout, now	ə	the schwa, an
â(r)	care, air	ŏŏ	took, full		unstressed vowel
ä	palm, father	ōō	pool, food		representing the
e	end, pet	u	up, done		sound spelled
ē	equal, tree	ŧ	her, sir,		*a* in *above*
i	it, give		burn, word		*e* in *sicken*
ī	ice, write	yōō	fuse, few		*i* in *possible*
o	odd, hot	z	zest, wise		*o* in *melon*
ō	open, so				*u* in *circus*
ô	order, jaw				

Acknowledgements

For permission to reprint copyrighted material, grateful acknowledgment is made to the following sources:

Into the Volcano by Donna O'Meara, photographs by Stephen and Donna O'Meara. Text © 2005 by Donna O'Meara. Photographs © by Stephen James O'Meara and Donna O'Meara. Reprinted by permission of Kids Can Press Ltd., Toronto. <www.kidscanpress.com>

from *The Llama's Secret*, adapted by Argentina Palacios, illustration by Chris Reasoner. Copyright © 1993 by Troll Associates Inc. Reprinted by Scholastic Inc.

Ogbo: Sharing Life in an African Village by Ifeoma Onyefulu. Text TK

On This Spot by Susan E. Goodman, illustrated by Lee Christiansen. Text © 2004 Susan E. Goodman. Illustrations © 2004 Lee Christiansen. Used by permission of HarperCollins Publishers.

Snowflake Bentley by Jacqueline Briggs Martin, illustrated by Mary Azarian. Text © 1998 by Jacquelie Briggs Martin. Illustrations © 1998 by Mary Azarian. Reprinted by permission of Houghton Mifflin Company. All rights reserved.

A Symphony of Whales by Steve Schuch, illustrated by Peter Sylvada. Text © 1999 by Steve Schuch. Illustrations © 1999 by Peter Sylvada. Reprinted by permission of Harcourt, Inc.

from *Thundercake* by Patricia Polacco. Copyright © 1990 by Patricia Polacco. Used by Permission of Philomel Books, a division of Penguin Young Readers Group, a member of Penguin Group (USA) Inc., 345 Hudson Street, New York, NY 10014. All rights reserved.

True Heart by Melissa Moss, illustrations by C. F. Payne. Text © 1999 by Marissa Moss. Illustrations © 1999 by C. F. Payne. Reprinted by permission of Harcourt, Inc.

Unit Opener Acknowledgements

P.2a Copyright Grandma Moses Properties Co. Location/Private Collection Edward Owen/Art Resource, NY; p.64a Fisk University/Alfred Stieglitz Collection; p.126a Central Park, ca. 1914-15 Maurice Brazil Prendergast (American [b. Newfoundland], 1858-1924)/The Metropolitan Museum of Art; p.188a Erich Lessing/Art Resource, NY.

Illustration Acknowledgements

P.12a Rob Doe/Wilkinson Studios; p.16c George Hamblin/Wilkinson Studios; p.16d George Hamblin/Wilkinson Studios; p.22b Burgandy Beam/Wilkinson Studios; p.24a Karel Hayes/Wilkinson Studios; p.28a Deborah Gross/Wilkinson Studios; p.30a Deborah Gross/Wilkinson Studios; p.32a, b Deborah Gross/Wilkinson Studios; p.46a Rowan Barnes-Murphy/Wilkinson Studios; p.47a Rowan Barnes-Murphy/Wilkinson Studios; p.48a Rowan Barnes-Murphy/Wilkinson Studios; p.49a Rowan Barnes-Murphy/Wilkinson Studios; p.49a Rowan Barnes-Murphy/Wilkinson Studios; p.50a Rowan Barnes-Murphy/Wilkinson Studios; p.51d Rowan Barnes-Murphy/Wilkinson Studios; p.54a Judith Hunt/Wilkinson Studios; p.56d Jim Kilmartin/Wilkinson Studios; p.58a Wendy Rassmusen/Wilkinson Studios; p.59a Wendy Rassmusen/Wilkinson Studios; p.60a Wendy Rassmusen/Wilkinson Studios; p.61a Wendy Rassmusen/Wilkinson Studios; p.62a Wendy Rassmusen/Wilkinson Studios; p.71b Rob Doe/Wilkinson Studios; p.74a Sergi Camara/Wilkinson Studios; p.78a Tammy Smith/Wilkinson Studios; p.80a Tammy Smith/Wilkinson Studios; p.82a Tammy Smith/Wilkinson Studios; p.84c George Hamblin/Wilkinson Studios; p.88b David Sheldon/Wilkinson Studios; p.88c David Sheldon/Wilkinson Studios; p.90a Sheila Bally/Wilkinson Studios; p.92a Sheila Balley/Wilkinson Studios; p.94a Sheila Balley/Wilkinson Studios; p. 104 Al Lorenz/Wilkinson Studios; p.106c George Hamblin/Wilkinson Studios; p.108a Dan Grant/Wilkinson Studios; p.110a Dan Grant/Wilkinson Studios; p.112a Dan Grant/Wilkinson Studios; p.113b Dan Grant/Wilkinson Studios; p.116a Dennis Franzen/Wilkinson Studios; p.121d Tony Boisvert/Wilkinson Studios; p.122c Tony Boisvert/Wilkinson Studios; p.122c Tony Boisvert/Wilkinson Studios; p.124c, d Tony Boisvert/Wilkinson Studios; p.132a, b Denny Bond/Wilkinson Studios; p.136a, b Tim Jones/Wilkinson Studios; p.150b, c, d Robert Eberz/Wilkinson Studios; p.152a Don Dyen/Wilkinson Studios; p.154a Don Dyen/Wilkinson Studios; p.156a Don Dyen/Wilkinson Studios; p.157b Don Dyen/Wilkinson Studios; p.167a Thomas Gagliano/Wilkinson Studios; p.168a Thomas Gagliano/Wilkinson Studios; p170a Tom McNeely/Wilkinson Studios; p.171a Tom McNeely/Wilkinson Studios;

p.172a Tom McNeely/Wilkinson Studios; p.174a Tom McNeely/Wilkinson Studios; p.176b, d Dave McPeek/Wilkinson Studios; p.177c Dave McPeek/Wilkinson Studios; 178a Jenny Sylvaine/Wilkinson Studios; p.183b, b, d, d Jeff Grunewald/Wilkinson Studios; p.184a, d Jeff Grunewald/Wilkinson Studios; p.186a Jeff Grunewald/Wilkinson Studios; p.187b Jeff Grunewald/Wilkinson Studios; p.198a, b Reggie Holladay/Wilkinson Studios; p.200a Robert Roper/Wilkinson Studios; p.204b George Hamblin/Wilkinson Studios; p.208d Jared Osterhold/Wilkinson Studios; p.210a Jerry Tiritilli/Wilkinson Studios; p.211a Jerry Tiritilli/Wilkinson Studios; p.214a Don Dyen/Wilkinson Studios; p.215a Don Dyen/Wilkinson Studios; p.216a Don Dyen/Wilkinson Studios; p.217a Don Dyen/Wilkinson Studios; p.218a Don Dyen/Wilkinson Studios; p.219b Don Dyen/Wilkinson Studios; p.229d George Hamblin/Wilkinson Studios; p.230a Dan Bridy/Wilkinson Studios; p.231b Dan Bridy/Wilkinson Studios; p.232a, c Drew Rose/Wilkinson Studios; p.234a Drew Rose/Wilkinson Studios; p.235a, d Drew Rose/Wilkinson Studios; p.236a Drew Rose/Wilkinson Studios; p.237b Drew Rose/Wilkinson Studios; p.240a Karel Hayes/Wilkinson Studios; p.242a, b, c, d K.E. Lewis/Wilkinson Studios; p.242d K.E. Lewis/Wilkinson Studios; p.245c George Hamblin/Wilkinson Studios.

Photography Acknowledgements

P.135 Element Photo Shoot; p.8d ©Rebecca Layton/Pediatric Community mural Project: The Healing Mural Woodhull Medical Center; Brooklyn, NY (Child Life Program, Pediatrics, and Groundswell Community Mural Project); p.11c Element Photo Shoot; p.26a, b ©Element Photo Shoot; p.41c Element Photo Shoot; p.44a Element Photo Shoot; p.70a Element Photo Shoot; p.76a Element Photo Shoot; p.77b Element Photo Shoot; p.86c, d Element Photo Shoot; p.87d Element Photo Shoot; p.106a Element Photo Shoot; p.118c Element Photo Shoot; p.150a Element Photo Shoot; p.162a Element Photo Shoot; p.165c Element Photo Shoot; p.166a Element Photo Shoot; p.197d Element Photo Shoot; p.227c Element Photo Shoot; p.228a Element Photo Shoot; p.4b ©Ariel Skelley/Corbis, AP; p.8a ©our-communitymural-l Xavier Cortada; p.14a ©Andy Crawford/Dorling Kindersley; p.14b ©Paul A. Souders/Corbis; p.15b ©Associated Press, AP; p.16b ©Associated Press, Enid News & Eagle; p.17d ©Associated Press, Anchorage Daily News; p.18b © Associated Press, AP 2nd Usage; p.18c ©Associated Press, Ames Tribune; p.19d © Copyright NBAE 2006. NBAE/Getty Images; p.20b© Dennis MacDonald/Alamy; p.20c ©Associated Press, AP; p.20d © Bob Rowan; Progressive Image/Corbis; p.21b ©Associated Press, Ames Tribune; p.22c ©Bettmann/Corbis; p.22d ©James L. Amos/Corbis; p.26c ©Pep Roig/Alamy; p.26d ©Associated Press, Daily Sitka Sentinel; p.27b ©Basket1 Marilyn Angel Wynn/Nativestock.com; p.33b ©Dorling Kindersley; p.34b ©Michael Newman/Photo Edit; p.38b ©Danny Lehman/Corbis; p.38d ©Eastcott Momatiuk/Getty Images; p.39c ©nmexicostamp U.S. Postal Service; p.39c ©alaskastamp U.S. Postal Service; p.42a ©Fabrice Coffini/epa/Corbis; p.42d ©Associated Press, AP; p.42b ©Images.com/Corbis; p.43c ©Sean Gardner/Reuters/Corbis; p.44b ©Laurie Vogt Photography Inc./Stockfood America; p.44c ©Burke/Triolo Productions/PictureQuest; p.44d ©David Bishop/PictureQuest; p.45d ©Lew Robertson/Stockfood; p.52a ©Earl & Nazima Kowall/Corbis; p.52b, c ©Associated Press, AP; p.53d ©Douglas St.Denny/Index Stock Imagery; p.56a ©James Nazz/Corbis; p.56b © Bettmann/Corbis; p.63b ©John White Photos/Alamy; p.66a ©Iconica/Flying Colours/Getty Images; p.70b ©Mike Powell/Corbis; p.83b ©Visual Arts Library (London)/Alamy; p.100b ©Eunice Harris/Index Stock Imagery; p.114a ©Photographer's Choice/Malcolm Fife/Getty Images; p.114d ©Time & Life Pictures/BOB Gomel/Getty Images; p.118a ©Bettmann/Corbis; p.120a ©Getty Images; p.122a ©Salvatore Vasapolli/Animals Animals – Earth Scenes; p.122c ©FEG Ben Shepard's Image of Sky WindPower Corporation's demonstration Flying Electric Generator; p124b ©Carlos Dominguez/CORBIS; p.128a ©Bettmann/Corbis; p.128b ©David Lyons/Alamy; p.132d ©Marco Solis/Alamy; p.138a ©Getty Images; p.138d ©DK Images/Lindsey Stock; p.140a ©The Print Collector/Alamy; p.141b ©Bettmann/Corbis 2nd usage; p.142d ©Getty Images; p.143b ©Time & Life Pictures/Getty Images; p.144b ©National Portrait Gallery, Smithsonian Institution/Art Resource, NY; p.144d ©Wally McNamee/Corbis; p.145b ©Wally McNamee/Corbis; p.146c ©Lester Lefkowitz/Getty Images; p.146d ©H. Armstrong Roberts/Corbis; p.147b ©Jeff Greenberg/Photo Edit; p.148a ©SSPL/The Image Works; p.148d ©Getty Images; p.151b ©John D. Rockefeller, Jr. Library; p.158c ©Leisurepix/Alamy; p.162b ©Free Agents Limited/Corbis; p.162b ©Trinette Reed/zefa/Corbis; p.163d ©JR Tokai/Reuters/Corbis; p.166d ©Corbis; p.167d ©Associated Press, AP; p.168d ©Gabe Palmer/Corbis; p.175b ©Firefly Productions/Corbis; p.180b ©Leisurepix/Alamy 2nd usage; p.180c ©Neil McAllister/Alamy; p.180d ©Courtesy of NASA; p.181b ©Kevin Fleming/Corbis; p.182b ©Courtesy of Berkeley Library; p.182d ©Kim Sayer/Corbis; p.194a ©Roger Ressmeyer/Corbis; p.194d ©Douglas Peebles/Corbis; p.194b©G Brad Lewis/GettyImages; p.195d ©Frans Lanting/Minden Pictures; p.201b ©Zephyr/Photo Researchers, Inc.; p.202a ©Christer Fredriksson/lonelyplanetimages.com; p.202b ©John Noble/Corbis; p.202c ©Panoramic Images/Getty Images; p.203a ©Martin Van Lokven/Foto Natura/Minden Pictures; p.203b ©Sandra Nykerk; p.204a ©age fotostock/SuperStock; p.205d ©age fotostock/SuperStock; p.206a ©Kevin R. Morris/Corbis; p.206b ©John Noble/Corbis 2nd ©Joe McDonald/Visuals Unlimited usage; p.206c ©Ric Ergenbright/Corbis; p.206d ©Joe McDonald/Visuals Unlimited; p.207d ©Dave King/Dorling Kindersley; p.208a ©Reuters/Corbis; p.208c ©3Sinks lo Tom Scott/ Florida Geological Survey/Department of Environmental Protection; p.209b ©Craig Lovell/Corbis; p.212a ©AFP / Getty Images; p.212c ©Vince Cavataio/Pacific Stock; p.213d ©Associated Press, AP; p.224a ©Gerry Ellis/Minden Pictures; p.224d ©Mark Raycroft/Minden Pictures; p.225c ©Frank Greenaway/Getty Images; p.228d ©John Sevigny/epa/Corbis; p.238b ©George Hall/Corbis; p.238c ©David Sailors/Corbis; p.243b ©Jim Zuckerman/Corbis; p.245b ©William Waterfall/Pacific Stock; p.246b ©Galen Rowell/Corbis; p.246d ©Kevin Schafer/Corbis; p.247b ©Hans Strand/Corbis; p.247d ©Chris Simpson/Getty Images; p.248b ©Jim Reed/Corbis; p.248d ©Jim Reed/Corbis; p.249b ©Jim Reed / Photo Researchers, Inc.

Additional Photography by Corbis/Harcourt Index; Photodisc/Getty Images/Harcourt Index; Getty Images/PhotoDisc/Harcourt Index; Kingvald/Dreamstime.com 2nd usage; Royalty-Free/Corbis; stephen mulcahey/Shutterstock.com; Marcaux/Dreamstime.com; Mdyson1/Dreamstime.com; Hway Kiong Lim/2003-2006 Shutterstock, Inc; photos.com; aaaah!/shutterstock; Photodisc Red/Bryan Mullennix/Getty Images; Photodisc Red/Getty Royalty Free Images; Stockdisc Classic/Getty Images; Masterfile Royalty Free Div/www.masterfile.com; Florea Marius Catalin/shutterstock 2nd usage; Brian Eastham/shutterstock; ablestock.com/Jupiterimages; Hemera Technologies/Alamy; Mschalke/Dreamstime.com; Photodisc/Getty Images/Telescope; PhotoDisc/ Everyday Living/Telescope; Eyewire/Telescope; Getty Images Royalty

Free/Telescope; FEMA News Photo/Telescope.